Guthrie's Lot Part 3:

The Crying Tree

Olwyn Harris

Reading Stones Publishing

Published by: Reading Stones Publishing
        Helen Brown & Wendy Wood
Cover Design: Wendy Wood

For more copies contact the publisher at:

Glenburnie Homestead
212 Glenburnie Road
ROB ROY NSW 2360
Mobile: 0422 577 663
Email: hbrown19561@gmail.com

For Helen, my sister, who took my drafts of
tears and translated them to tangible pages.
Thank you for being part of this journey!

The Crying Tree

"You have kept count of my sleepless tossings; you have collected
my tears in your bottle.
Are they not recorded in your book?"

(Psalm 56:18)

Olwyn Harris

2010

1.

She threw the photograph down onto her drafting table and leaned back in her chair. Keith Tomlin looked at her and shook his head. "So, it's not heritage listed... and it is not condemned? Are you sure?"

"Come on, Tommy. I wouldn't be doing this if I hadn't done my homework. Of course, it's condemned! But look at these stone walls. They are magic. The engineer who inspected it said they're as solid as the day they were made. It's perfect".

He pulled up a chair. "Okay. Tell me. When are you doing this hair-brained scheme? It hardly seems like you, Mac."

She shrugged in a melancholy sort of way. "Nothing seems like me anymore. That's the point: this is the prescription. My doctor has been pushing me to take time off. Tommy, I've got to take a break, and this seems more like me than sunbaking in the Maldives."

"So how long do you reckon you'll need?" He started calculating the cost: to his staff, to his clients, to his bottom-line.

She grimaced. "I've got plenty of leave. So maybe... four... six months?" But she quickly went on. "But it's not as bad as it sounds..." Once the studio was functional, she fully intended to get back to work. They could send her jobs… and besides, it just made sense to supervise the work in person. "You never know, shovelling dirt could be quite therapeutic." She smiled in a charming, nothing-will-change-my-mind way. She picked up the photo. "I will have a country retreat where I can go on weekends… or take a week out here or there. It's just like your hut… but rural. You might find I will do my best creative work out there."

He sighed. "You know we've got that Smythe job coming up. If you're going away, I might have to give it to Reg." He glanced across at her.

She was looking intently at the photograph in her hand and didn't even glance up. "Colonoscopy-boy will be happy about that."

He shook his head. Hmm. Okay… she didn't take the bait. Perhaps she was sincere about needing a break. "Dare I ask…?"

"Oh, come on. He's a right pain in the you-know-where. All he has ever delivered is… well, basically only worth flushing. He hasn't shown one original idea in the entire time he's been here. Tommy you've made the mark of this place *creative*. You know he hasn't got it."

Keith smiled in spite of himself. "Guess that's one of the joys of being the boss with less options. Reg's keen to prove himself."

"He's keen to *promote* himself. He's been preening and posturing and positioning since he got here." She shrugged. "Guess this is his break." Really, she couldn't care less. If performance was anything to go on, he was hardly a threat.

Something in his throat constricted and Keith glared at her severely. "You look after yourself kiddo. And get back here as soon as you can. I don't want to lose you, Mac."

"Yes Boss. Besides, I'll be on the phone. I'm not dying." And she grimaced and turned away. "Damn it!" she muttered as she swiped at her eyes. "I really have to do this."

ೲ෮ಌೞ

Mac pulled up in her convertible and waited for the dust to clear. It had been an exhilarating drive: the top down blowing the cobwebs away as she followed the white lines, streaming the last two horrendous years behind her. Sure, they had been about her mum but there were times when she thought it would kill her too.

Right now, this project was a marking stone: a monument to change. If she did this properly, then her life could go back to the way it was, when it was creative energy, and driven targets, and focused passion. All the prep stuff was out of the way, so now the real fun could start, and she knew she would not be able to stop until it was finished. "You're like a dog with a bone," Keith said more than once. He even went so far as to suggest Mac stood for the bulldog cast sitting on the bonnet of a Mack truck. Huh. Well, who knew? Perhaps it did. It got the job done.

She stepped out of the car and stood at the tumble-down gate, rusted, and bent, the scrolled iron limp from age. She pulled out her phone and took a photo. This was her gate now... tumbled down did not matter. It was hers, inviting her into a different place... space... pace. Now she was here, it was begging her to get started.

Wire and grass and rubble did nothing to dampen her excitement. She was a visionary. This was Mac's genius. She could see the whole thing. Fresh, new, incorporating those incredibly old, irreplaceable stone-walls; to create a space that, for once, was just for her, and not some trendy, double income couple who had more money and social self-importance than was healthy.

It was a five-hectare block, and she was determined to live on site right from the start. It was screaming for her to add her own footprint. She wasn't going to pay rent and a mortgage.   The demountable donga had already been delivered out the back. A portable bathroom – the loo and a shower – that was being delivered today. When she told Tommy about that he had laughed so hard. He could not imagine it at all, so Mac had painstakingly explained the practicality of having a separate facility that would be available for the work crew as well. She wasn't having tradesmen traipsing through her private quarters to use the dunny. She checked her watch and stepped over the broken fence. She paced out the front yard, through a tangle of grass, and wandered to the side to take more photos from another angle. Building was going to be her therapy: hammers and nails and paintbrushes. All hands on, just like those reality shows without the dramatic time-stressed competition, or the incompatible personalities, or clashing wills and stale ideas. This was going to work so well. But first things first. Today was for settling into the donga, internet, and a shower.

She wandered around the site, considering what was salvageable. A lizard hissed and scuttled away. She jumped. She had to admit there didn't seem much left worthy of recycling. Apart from the stone, most things had succumbed to the ravages of time. There were a few pieces of interesting rusting iron, and the beams may be okay for panelling garden walls, or paths, and some boards that could probably add character as a feature here or there, like in the chook-yard. Yes. A hen-house: that was her folly in this project. Every project she added a "folly": just like the classical masters. Even something small or symbolic. It was her way of having fun, adding her private signature. Some clients scorned it, but she included it in the plan anyway.

Her mum had treasured a faded childhood photo of her holding one of her aunt's Plymouth-rock hens: plump, speckled, and homely. They were a lot like her mum really. Not that she knew anything about chooks. She had to go to a speciality breeder and place an order.

She frowned and rechecked her watch. Seriously? The delivery was late. She mentally readjusted her timetable. She'd just grab a bite from the servo on the corner in town. Plenty of time to do grocery shopping tomorrow. She took a deep breath. Plenty of time. Period. There was no corporate timetable; no tightly scheduled tradesmen; no crabby clients breathing down her neck. She could afford to take it slowly. This was the point. She had six months, and it was just one small studio cottage. Hopefully, if all went well, she could take the last couple of months of that period and luxuriate in the prescription of taking a break. No pressure. No demands. She couldn't wait.

2.

Mac went back and sat in her car, the radio humming its usual white noise of social banter. She checked the time again and peered out at the cloudy skyline that was darkening in the late afternoon light. She pulled out a folder and checked a phone number and dialled. There was no answer. She got out and looked down the road. She sat back in the driver's seat, drumming her fingers against the steering wheel. She bounced out again and strode around the back, pacing out the position of the studio; double-checking that she had free access for construction around it. Finally, she heard the grinding of gears as a truck drove up the gravel road.

She strode forward. The truck pulled in, spewing dust over her. She was ready with a copy of their quote and delivery time; and her chequebook. The driver opened the door and jumped down. He was stocky and wore short shorts. He had a quick smile hidden behind reddish hair that flopped in his eyes. He looked over at her, standing near her little low car in high heels, phone in hand, and braced himself. "Afternoon," he said casually. "Delivery for Macintosh?"

"Yes, that's me. The arranged time was two-thirty."

He shrugged apologetically. "Got held up. Traffic accident. Sorry for the wait." He'd learnt a long time ago: ascribe responsibility to a tragedy outside your control, look contrite for the inconvenience and don't hang around. "But show me where you want this, and I'll get it unloaded. Guess you'll want to get on with your day."

"Guess my day is just about over." He ignored her snipe and indicated the front yard. She was prompt to clarify, "No, not here. It goes out the back. Near the demountable."

He had a quick look around and jumped back in the cab. He reversed in, and skilfully manoeuvred into place. He climbed out, undid the chains, and looked very busy. He had no intention of talking. Not to this one. He operated the crane with great concentration and dumped it just a little hard. The cubical was quickly unloaded. "There you go." He wrote out the delivery paperwork and handed her the invoice. "Understand the boss said you were paying on delivery."

This was her opening. "Well normally, yes. But I have been greatly inconvenienced and the contractual arrangement has not been adhered to. I'll pay for the delivery and deduct the waiting time."

He raised his eyebrows and smirked just a little. "Really? You're just not going to pay?"

"I am going to pay. Just not the full amount. My time is valuable, even if yours is not. Standard procedure for my firm."

"Are you sure? I mean I will have to check with the boss about this..."

"I have no doubt at all." She checked the invoice and calculated the amount she needed to write on the cheque.

She intentionally kept the payment old-school to assert her feeling of control.

"Fair enough..." He rolled his eyes and stepped away. He dialled a number and waited for an answer. He mumbled a bit; paused and sighed. "Sure. See ya then." She couldn't hear exactly what was said and really, she had no interest. She had got her way. She usually did.

He came back and shrugged. He said nothing as he reattached the straps around the base of the loo. He had it fully suspended when she appeared with the cheque in her hand.

"What on earth are you doing?" she demanded. "Touched base with the boss – like I said. He's really sorry for the inconvenience, but he reckons that for a full delivery, the full amount is in order. He said if that isn't suitable, you can find another carrier. I did ask if you were sure. You said, you were sure. Don't take you for a lady who would change your mind... so I will be out of your way real soon."

"You're taking the bathroom?"

"Sure. Full payment on delivery. Boss said you were clear about the terms."

"At a particular time, you might note. That was not adhered to. It voids the contract."

"Yeah – sorry about that. Traffic is outside my control." He had no qualms regarding his creative use of fictitious commuter pileups.

"Traffic!" She looked like she was going to explode. He pressed the button and resumed loading. His bet was that she would not give in easily. He'd seen her type: urban, testy, ambitious, with something to prove. Well, it didn't prove anything to him whether she had her little spat or not. He had started testing the tension the straps around the cubicle when she really understood he would soon drive away.

"You can't just take it. I need it, or I would not have ordered it. I'm not going through all this again."

"A-huh." He checked the anchorages were firmly attached.

"How can you just drive away? You've come all the way down here; spent the money on fuel and wages. You would be better to narrow your margin and take my payment!"

He just smiled and shrugged. "Hmm? Great advice, but that isn't my call. The boss says... well, you know what he said."

"But I've been waiting around all afternoon!"

"Well, Ms Macintosh," he said mildly without even a hint of resentment, "I trust your next carrier will have more consideration. I'll make a note if you like, so the office staff don't take any more of your jobs. That shouldn't be too hard – I make my own bookings."

She was not fooled. "You're blacklisting me? That is outrageous!"

"Well, let's see," and now Ned was seriously starting to enjoy himself. "I look at it more as a gesture of courtesy since our service has been so totally disappointing for you."

"I will make sure that you never get any of my work again!" Mac boiled and glared.

He shook his head in mock sadness and spoke slowly. "Gee... tough." He brightened as he went back to work. "Only, I remember there's only been this one job, and you haven't wanted to pay on that. This softens the blow some. Well, as they say: this is Gumleigh... and this is Gumleigh General Carrying... at your service." He nodded and strode towards the cab and climbed up.

"You can't take it!" she spluttered.

He wound down the window and gave a friendly wave. "Just take it up with the boss. Number is on the invoice."

He ground the gears and drove away slowly. He looked in the rear vision mirror and jolted the brakes to stir up the dust. She wasn't moving. "Come on..." he urged through gritted teeth, as he turned on the indicator at the intersection. Just then the phone rang. He pulled over, more dust flying. "Gumleigh General Carrying, Ned speaking... Oh, Ms Macintosh," he said as if he wasn't expecting her call at all. "Yeah, sure. No, I didn't get too far at all. I'll be right there." And he paused just a little while, grinning triumphantly, before finding somewhere to turn around and he drove back.

Mac stood in front of the cabin and sighed. This would have to go down in the annals of her life as a particularly humiliating day. It was not very often she didn't win.

At least she had salvaged the convenience of a bathroom. But when she opened the cubical there was a very vacant space where the shower should have been. There was only a toilet. No shower? She tried to ring the hire-place to find out why a functioning toilet-shower combo wasn't sent, and only got an answering service.

By the time she went down to the servo, they had closed the kitchen and were not serving any hot food, so she bought a coffee, a packet of chips, and a chocolate bar. Dinner. She showered at the truck-stop facilities and cringed during the whole operation. By the time she was done she felt like she needed fumigating which defied the logic of having the shower in the first place. Having a bathroom at her site was not an optional extra.

Mac stepped into the demountable and walked around the prefab kitchen-laundry and turned on a tap. There was a soft dry squeak as she turned it off again. How long would it be before she could get water? She sat in the middle of the empty floor and ate her chips. Flicking through Facebook entries on her phone for distraction, and she was about halfway through the chocolate bar when she stopped chewing and stared at the bare window. Her backside was numb, and her nerves stretched. She suddenly realised that she had no bed... no mattress... no camp-stretcher. She'd thrown in a sleeping bag at the last minute without a thought. That's all she had... and she was really tired. Her luggage consisted of essentials such as hairdryer and coffee maker and steam iron. If that idiot delivery driver hadn't been late, she would not have been so distracted and realised sooner. Now it was impossible to do anything about it. She took some deep breaths to settle her indignation. Never mind, she was going to have to take that motel room after all.

3.

Mac woke to someone tapping on her car window. "Hello? Are you okay?"

She startled and jolted upright, banging her elbow, her head throbbing and her pride smarting. She pushed aside the sleeping bag and wound down the window. "What?" She looked smack bang into a pair of jeans and a leather belt-buckle.

He stepped back and turned around, facing the other way. "I was to meet a... someone Macintosh, about the building job... around eight o'clock. I waited in town. It's eight-thirty."

She clambered for her phone, to check the time and prove him wrong. The phone was flat... no alarm. She ran her hand through her short hair, and quickly checked it the rear-vision mirror. She looked like death.

She closed her eyes and took a breath. There was no way she was giving Tommy the pleasure of seeing her crawl back defeated. She would do this, however humiliating it became. Couldn't get any worse than yesterday.

She found her shoes and unfolded herself from the car. Her collar was crooked, and her long pants twisted. She stuck out her hand. "I'm Mac. Sorry about that. My phone's flat." She tried to inconspicuously straighten herself out.

He grinned. He was clearly a man used to manual work. "Gumleigh has a motel," he said as he shook her hand.

"Humph. They're renovating and there were no rooms left last night. I had no notion that I'd need a reservation in a place like this."

"Oh," he said making very little effort to suppress a smile. "...a place like this?" Huh. Ned had been right.

"Besides, I had been planning on setting up in the demountable. The delivery was so late I had no time to run in and buy a mattress."

"Oh? You were just going to run in..."

"Yes."

"...and buy a mattress?"

"Of course. I'm just saying..."

"Sure," he said cutting in. "Look. I have another job I've got to get back to, so why don't we grab a coffee at the servo, and we can go over the details... and see if you've got any concerns. I have until nine-fifteen." He walked over to his ute and got in. She went to say something, but realised he'd already started to drive off.

She scrambled around and flushed out her keys. She plugged in her phone, hoping to get a slight charge back on it. And followed the dust towards town. This was a nightmare.

Daniel Henry walked into the service station with an easy smile. "Mornin' Snooks. Need two coffees..."

The lady behind the counter had greying hair and an uninviting sort of line to her mouth. "Want anything to eat?"

"Yeah. Just eggs and toast; side of bacon, for me. Not sure about the other one," he said, indicating over his shoulder.

She looked through the door as Mac's car pulled in beside his ute. "Oh... Miss Skim-latte-no-sugar-with-a-shot-of-caramel... 'cept we don't do caramel. Thought she was going to torch the place last night. We'd already cleaned out the bain-marie."

He grinned. "Just plain skim then. And some extra toast. Is Bob around? I need to put up the order..."

"Nah – he's over at the shop already. Pam's off again and couldn't open up."

"No worries, I'll catch him there. Thanks," he said, as he took the coffees and sat by the window. He pulled out his pad, and his phone and scrolled through his diary, making notes. He watched Mac cutting through the café, making a beeline for the Ladies. His phone rang and he answered. "Hey Ned. How's it going?" He chuckled as he listened. "Nah, that'd spoil your fun; twisted as it is. Sure. Yep – at the Motel all day. Just checking in with that job now. No, you're right... she seems pretty up-tight." They chatted for bit, and he hung up grinning as Mac walked over and sat down. She had changed her shirt, washed her face and teeth, and smelt like peppermint.

He pushed her coffee towards her. It seemed to Mac that he was throwing her a bone. Well, she wasn't going to let her guard down. She clambered to regain her footing.

This wasn't a good start. "So, you're a difficult man to get hold of. It seems strange that we are only just meeting now..."

He took a breath. "So then. Let me introduce myself... properly. I'm Dan Henry."

Mac took his hand and shook it firmly. "And I'm Mac. Thank you."

"Mac?" He looked at her. "Just Mac?"

"Some friends call me C-C." She looked outside through the glass panelling. That's what her dad would call her, and she used it on her social profile page. She couldn't remember the last time she answered the phone, and someone actually called her 'C-C'. That was telling.

"C-C?"

"My initials. You can call me Mac."

"Right. Okay then." He paused and drank some of his coffee. "Well, I've looked over your plans again. What you want to do is interesting."

"Interesting?" That was insulting. She raised her right eyebrow. "You have doubts you can do this? If you have any concerns Mr Henry, then perhaps you'd better let me know so I can source another contractor from the start. I have no inclination to be switching halfway through the job."

He looked at her. She was wound as tight as a coil spring ready to pop. Dan nodded to Snooks as she handed him his bacon and eggs. He passed the extra side of toast over to Mac. "You can have that if you want. I'm eating since I'm on a break." She stared at him as he generously sprinkled salt on his eggs. And then went for the pepper. He was stalling, and he knew it. He prayed quietly under his breath, while studying his eggs intently. "I really don't want this job if it's going to be more trouble than it's worth. Certainly not paying great. What do you think? Your call."

He put down his knife and fork and reached for his coffee. His mouth went grim as he drank, and quietly continued his internal dialogue of silent prayer. "Figured you'd say that. Consider the job a tithe. And I'll have to work up to the 'cheerful giving' part. Not there yet." He closed his eyes and took another breath, and then looked into her face. "I thought it was interesting, not because I can't do it; but because I wouldn't have thought of doing it that way myself: interesting."

"So, you like it?"

She wasn't asking... more like demanding. She reminded him of his nephew, running in when he had mastered a new move on his scooter petitioning applause. "Well, it's... interesting," he said noncommittally. "Guess it depends on what you want to do with it as to how functional it will be. I lean towards functional myself."

"Yeah... it's a little bit Samuel Mockbee. But his whole point is you can have functional and interesting." She cringed. 'Interesting' was not part of her vocabulary. "I prefer to think of it as art with a practical edge... something with both dimensions." She felt the pitch of her voice rise a notch.

"As to function, I'm looking for a studio retreat where I can come to work when I need a break. Functionally, it is perfect."

"You're working on creating a work-space so you can get away from work, to do more work?" He laughed. "Sounds like me. Not sure how healthy it is though."

She relaxed just a little as she watched his eyes. "Well, if you are that committed, we may be able to satisfactorily work together after all." To her it sealed the deal. She'd done her research; she'd looked over buildings he'd constructed; the execution of his work was good. They'd spoken on the phone a number of times. She had no doubts. She hardly paused. "I had a look at the break down on your scope of work. The quote is fairly lean, but it seems that the simplest way to condense this for me, is that I do as much of the hands-on labouring as I can. I'm here for six months max, and I'm going to be living on site so I can use every available moment. Right now, my priority is plumbing and power on the demountable. Oh, and, if you could point me to the local furniture shop, I'll have to get some basics."

He looked sceptically at her slight frame. But it was more her giant sized ego that had him wondering. It took a fairly audacious type to hire themselves for a job. Arrogant actually. He had his standard labouring contacts. Could he work with someone who was so opinionated? He shrugged. He sincerely doubted she would make the distance, but even if she did, it wasn't a huge job, so the risk was not great. Besides, local jobs were not so easy to come by. Not having to travel again for a while, that was a plus. "Hmm? And just how is that going to work? You'd be working for me, even though you're my boss? Sounds messy to me."

"I'm sure it'll be fine," she said matter-of-factly, "We are both professionals," and she went back to her coffee and toast. She was hungry.

He cleared his throat and said, "Well, I have never done that before: using an owner/architect for labour hire on a project. What's involved is a bit different to building a kit-shed."

"I know perfectly well what is involved! There is absolutely no resemblance to a farm shed!"

"Guess that's my point. I'll tell you what: I'll give it a shot on a couple of conditions." He waited for her to look directly at him. "We'll try it in fortnightly blocks... re-evaluate every couple of weeks. At any time either of us can pull the pin."

She shrugged. It was a done deal. She would say whatever would make him get on with it.

"Also, you clock on and clock off like any labourer. I need someone there: not skipping off to buy nail-polish.

"You expect me to let that arrogantly sexist comment to go unchallenged, don't you?"

He shrugged and grinned. Wasn't that calling the kettle black! Still, she got the point. "I've got nothing against saving money, but I don't cut corners. If it isn't safe, or if I think it's going to be dodgy, I'll play a red card. And if I pull that out, it will be done my way: without exception. Mac, that's my rule.   Ultimately, it's my workmanship and reputation on display here... and believe me, people are watching. So, if you can't abide by that, you should probably let me use my own labour, or source your other contractor right now." He closed his eyes and prayed she would.

She took another bite of toast and didn't even hesitate. "Not half as much as this is show-casing my design. So, let me assure you up front that this is personal, and I won't be cutting corners for dodgy. There is not too much that is salvageable on the site: perhaps some iron, a few timbers that can be used for places that are not structural – landscaping and such. The stone walls must stay of course: they are the feature. They are the clincher on why I chose here. How soon can we clear the site to be ready for construction?"

He swallowed, disappointed. She was not going to back out gracefully. He opened up his diary and had a perverse inkling to be very busy for another three months. "Pretty sure your priority, plumbing and power, will be delayed, but I should be able to start in about four to five weeks." It was a fair assessment.

She had a mouth full of coffee and spluttered. "Five weeks! That's ridiculous. When we spoke on the phone, I made a booking. That was months ago."

"Tentative is tentative... and doesn't pay my bills. This is not my only job. Besides, like I said, last I spoke with Phillips he was booked solid for three weeks, so you won't get power until then at least."

"That's preposterous! What happened to the rural recession and tradesmen begging for work?"

"Come on, Mac, you've done this before. Why are you acting like this is the first time you've come across delays? It's the nature of the beast."

"You are so right. I have done this a million times before, and I have no intention of being stone-walled by tradies who think they can ride over me rough-shod just because I'm a size ten!"

He looked at her, bristled and hunched over her coffee and wondered how well she was going to fit in here. And that had nothing at all to do with her dress size. "I'm just not sure that barging in all testy and assuming I need the privilege of your work is the way to fix this." He spoke mildly, as if he was reading stock and bonds prices.

She stiffened and swigged the dregs of her café latté. She swallowed carefully, restraining every fibre in her body so she didn't tell him what she really thought of his character, his parentage, his upbringing, his education, or lack of it, and his overall deficiency in professionalism. "You took the job. I don't want mates' rates. I just expect a reasonable service at a reasonable price. And reliable. I need people to arrive when they say they will."

He chuckled. "I don't recall being late this morning."

"I... well, my phone was flat. It has never happened before, and it won't happen again. Seriously, I need to begin this sooner than what you're offering."

"Your place." He shrugged. "You can start whenever you want."

"I need a trade-help. I need it done right."

He looked at his phone and sighed. If it came to needs, he needed this as much as he needed a migraine. He dialled a number. "Phillips? Dan. Yeah. Starting that job out on Guthrie's Road... yeah, same place. Do you think we can get some power sooner? Ahuh." Then he rang the plumber and checked the time on his phone. It was already half past. "I've got to go shortly," he said as he drained his coffee and passed on the information from his calls. "I can tell you that I won't be finished my current job any earlier than I said. Guess I could come out in the afternoons after four, for a couple of hours, just to get you started..."

"Two hours?" she scoffed. "You make that sound like you are doing me a magnanimous favour."

"I am." Why didn't he just walk away?

Mac closed her eyes and bit her tongue. "Where did you say the furniture-shop was?"

"I didn't. Gumleigh doesn't have one."

"What do you mean?"

"Except for the Op-shop – there's no place to buy furniture. Well, there are some things at the hardware shop, but mostly you have to order in. There's a shopping centre in Blackstone. Not far... just forty-five minutes."

"That's ridiculous."

"That's the way it is."

"How do I get it from there to here?"

"I can recommend a local General Carrier." He opened his wallet and pushed over a business card.

"Ned the Neanderthal? No way."

He put down is phone and raised his eyebrows. He was amused. "Ned the Neanderthal?"

She went to drink her coffee and grimaced. Her cup was empty. "He was extremely rude and unprofessional."

"I, ahh... in fact, I've always considered Ned an easy guy to get along with." Dan noticed that her face flushed with indignation. She was still smarting.

"He was late and arrived with some cock-and-bull story about a road accident. I had the radio on all afternoon." Dan considered her. She ignored his obvious amusement. She was not duped. "Traffic reports are to commuters, as weather reports are to farmers. We live by them. And then, even after he unloaded it all, he reloaded the whole thing and was going to take it back with him."

Dan's smirk spread a little broader. "Now, why would he do that?"

"He told his boss I wasn't going to pay him. I was going to pay... just with a deduction for being late. It was entirely reasonable."

"Huh. His boss thought that not paying for the job was unreasonable?" His sarcastic bewilderment did not amuse her.

"Yes. No. Whatever. It was just a standard deduction. He told me to take it up with his obnoxious boss if I had any issues. I could tell he was enjoying the whole debacle."

"That I can believe..."

"It was very upsetting. So, no... I would rather not. Thank you." She pushed the card back across the table.

He shrugged and put it back in his wallet. "Well, will you?"

"Will I use Ned the general carrier? Not until Hell freezes over!"

"I was actually wondering if you were thinking of taking it up with his boss." His eyes laughed at her again. "The obnoxious one..."

"I've got a number of carefully selected things I would say to him, but I've better things to do with my time than to worry about someone like that. In the end, I paid so he would bring it back. Which made me even later, and I missed having dinner because everything was already closed."

Dan's grin broadened and he stood to his feet. "Well, if you ever change your mind about your carefully selected conversation with the obnoxious boss, I would love to be in on that."

"That's pathetic." Mac was irritated. "Who else in town delivers furniture?"

"Can't say I can recommend anyone else. I'll see you at four o'clock." He grabbed his phone and notebook and left.

꧁ ❧ ꧂

4.

Mac made a call to the furniture shops in Blackstone. Deliveries out of town incurred a fee. And from where she stood, it was a ridiculously exorbitant fee. "But if I bought a number of furniture items that you would normally deliver locally for free, logically an accumulation of purchases would add up to a trip to Gumleigh, don't you think?" They didn't think so and would not be moved. She wasn't going to go to all the trouble of packing up her unit for just six months. She had allocated the amount the removalist had quoted, to buy substitute furniture. She figured that would spare her the time and trouble. Nothing about rural-country was calm and relaxed – that was an urban-myth of epic proportions! Everything actually incurred delays and angst.

In the end, she went to the Gumleigh Salvation Army Op-shop and spent up big. She bought a second-hand bed and mattress, some linen, kitchen stuff, curtains, a small table, a couple of chairs, and a daybed. She negotiated with the shop assistant that if they delivered to the donga, they could have everything back when she was done with them in a few months, plus anything else she had acquired that wasn't needed. There was no negotiation really. They were there to help, as were the two amiable old codgers who delivered her goods. As they closed the door on their delivery truck, she felt compelled to give them a generous donation as well. She realised, as they drove off waving, that what she gave them covered the delivery fee from Blackstone. She shrugged. It wasn't that she begrudged the money; it was their we-won't-be-moved attitude that irked her. Besides, this way, she had not blown her entire budget on her temporary camp. The difference could go towards custom-made items when she outfitted the studio later on.

Afterwards, she went to the hardware shop. A tall man, with the usual middle-aged spread around his girth, was stacking paint-tins on a shelf. Mac walked around the shop in a sort of daze. How could a town without even a furniture shop have a well-stocked hardware store? She was relieved. It seemed everything she might need immediately would be here.   The man introduced himself, shaking her hand violently. "I'm Bob. I hear you're doing something with the old Guthrie place. About time something was done with it."

Mac returned his handshake warmly. She expected he would be surprised by what that 'something' was. "I am looking forward to getting started."

"Well, you've got Dan Henry on your job. Reckon he'll do good by you. His father worked his way up from being a lacky in the timber workshop to owning this whole joint. This town has this great little shop because of him. That's their style. Henrys are good people."

Mac bristled. Why was all this community confidence always weighted towards Mr Henry?   What about her contribution?   She had a reputation that was not to be sneezed at. Her work had been featured in professional and lifestyle publications so many times she gave up counting. Clients requested her work by name.

"Well, take a look around, Mac. Of course, Dan said he'd apply the trade discount to anything you need. He tells me you'll be labouring for him as well. Thought that was a hoot! Nice change from those types who come through here treating us like serfs. Expecting us to drop everything to cater to their pampered little notions." He pumped her hand again. "When I heard you were not afraid to pitch in and get a bit of dirt under your fingernails, well, I had a real good feeling about your time here at The Gums."

Mac blinked. Okay... he might not recognise her name, but he recognised her style: hard work and then more hard work. That was certainly her mark. It almost left the taste of joy in her mouth.

Bob grinned and continued, "Gotta say, I was kinda surprised though, since me Ol' Girl said you were a pretty little thing who wanted caramel in your coffee and just ate chocolate for dinner. Just goes to show... you can't tell."

Mac turned away. Enough already! She would have eaten more for her dinner if there had been more to eat. Still, she would certainly take advantage of the trade discount. She bought a barrow and started loading it with stuff. She added a lamp to the pile, a shovel and nail-rake, a couple of pairs of gloves and a hat. She wandered around and saw an out-door table setting. Finally, she was done. For the rest she would stay with her catalogues. When she walked past a generator for the third time, she asked Bob about it. "What sort of generator do you think... ahh, which one would Dan Henry choose?" It was awkward. She hadn't anticipated this delay on site power.

He looked at the model on the floor in disgust. "I know these reps think they are doing us favours bringing these dinky little things in here. This would be all right if you only want to charge your phone and keep a candle burning, but add anything else and you'd be straining that thing to the max. You choose the size by calculating your expected usage. And you know Dan, he has got some serious power tools. I'm thinking something with a bit more oomph, like this green one, might be what you'd be looking at." She sighed with relief knowing she could charge her phone, much less anything else. It was an expensive investment, and she was reassured that the green model was money well spent. "Now Mac, don't worry your pretty little head about getting this stuff up to your place. You wouldn't get it in your little car anyway. I'll let Dan know so he can run it up to your place later. He always drops in after work anyhow."

Mac let it ride. The condescension of someone organising her "pretty little" life was irritating, but just now she needed Bob on side. She went and bought some groceries and dropped in to picked up some lunch at the servo on her way back.

Snooks glared at her over her glasses, as she walked in. "Want a coffee?"

Mac nodded. "Want food?"

"Chicken wrap, no mayo."

Snooks said nothing until she handed her the coffee and lunch packet over the counter. "Bob said you went to the shop. That's agreeable... supporting local business like that. Kinda thought your sort would be catalogue people."

Mac just nodded as she pocketed her change. Her pile of catalogues, with a plethora of sticky-notes bookmarking ideas, was in a lined box at the donga waiting for her attention.

⚚⁊

When Dan pulled up that afternoon, Mac had already made her bed, packed the pantry, and hung curtains. It wasn't The Grand Marriott by any stretch of the imagination, but it would do. She was keen to get her fridge started and her phone charged. When she went outside, Dan was unloading his ute.

"This isn't the generator I bought. It's yellow."

"Nope. Swapped it. You have a fairly healthy credit at the store." He looked quite pleased with himself.

"You swapped it? Bob said he gave me a discount on the best one. You just can't go swapping things without talking to me."

"Well, I couldn't ring because your phone went to message, and since Bob said you asked about which one I would choose, I went that way. You're not trying to start your own power station here. This one is reliable and will do the job fine."

"But what about your power-tools? He said you needed..."

"You can take it back tomorrow if you like."

She frowned. "No, I guess not. Did Bob mind?"

"Nope. Don't reckon he minded at all." Her frown deepened when he went on to say with a smirk. "My power-tools have batteries." Dan watched her inhale the idea she had been sold something unnecessary. He shrugged and continued unloading. "Maybe he was being helpful. More likely just testing. He knows I'm looking out for you now, so he won't do it again."

"I don't need you looking out for me! I can handle myself thank you very much!"

Dan stopped himself from saying what was on the tip of his tongue and hauled the generator out behind the demountable. He wondered two things. One, did she want a response to that? And two, if he did respond, would he be honest or just keep it polite? Safer to say nothing. Considering he was going to have to work with her, and he had given his word on that, he figured polite was all she was going to get.

ƸӜƷ

5.

Dan hooked up the generator and gave Mac a couple of practice runs at getting it started. Twice she landed on her rear-end and had to pick herself up, giving him a flick as he made no effort to hide his amusement.

"I'll bring the bob-cat out once we've salvaged as much as we can. That'll get things moving." He looked at her curiously as Mac allowed her excitement to peek through unchecked with a delighted grin. "So, I'll see you tomorrow, I guess," he said.

Mac was actually starting to believe it was possible for the action proper to start soon. Everything had been going so slow. "Dan... umm. I wanted to ask..." She hesitated. "About... water."

Was she floundering? This was obviously uncomfortable for her. "What's the problem?"

"I don't have any... water."

"Plenty of underground water here. The original bore ran pretty well I believe, but it'd be a good idea to retest it. At home we run the bore for domestics and use rainwater for the kitchen and garden. Hard bore water wrecks the soil, kills your plants and tastes like cat-piss."

Mac was not listening. She felt her emotions start to spin. "Oh. Umm. Well, you see... therein lies a problem. I chose this cubical model because it had a toilet with a shower included, but this particular one has had the shower removed."

Dan looked at her, now openly amused. "Maybe you should have let Ned take it back."

"Don't be ridiculous. I need the toilet." She swallowed. "Anyway, I was, well... I was wondering if you could put up a shower for me to use until I can get it exchanged?"

"You want me to build you a camp shower?" She nodded.

"Well, I must admit that is a rather unusual request; but sure. That'll be an hourly rate. It won't be the Ritz though."

"I don't want the Ritz. I just want privacy and somewhere to shampoo my hair. Gumleigh Servo is hardly private." It was unbelievable that they couldn't exchange that cubical for at least another two weeks. She had never come up against so many roadblocks in her life.

"You're the architect. I'm not sure you'll be okay with something I would knock up, even temporarily."

"Are you serious? I don't 'design' cubicles out of corrugated iron and crossbeams to hang up a camp shower. But a shelf and a towel rail would be helpful. And somewhere to put my clothes, up out of the mud. I feel like I'm going back to my Grade Six bushwhacker camp."

"Okay – I'm thinking you're pretty set on what you want." He handed her his notepad. "Draw it so I have something to start with."

She regarded him dubiously, and then roughly sketched her concept. He looked at her hand deftly translating her thoughts onto paper and raised his brow. She was good. No doubt she had to be to hold her own in an industry that was very competitive.

"How about a traditional camp figuration for privacy?" And he scribbled over her lines. "Like this?" She cringed. No one drew over her work; even rudimentary site sketches. That was one of her rules. But this was his pad, so she could hardly snatch it back. He noticed her squirm. "A door requires a substantial structure to swing it. Which translates in extra time. For something temporary it may not be worth it."

"I'll go with the door... and it will be worth it," she said tersely, covering her embarrassment. "We could use the door off the old out-house. The main house has collapsed but that toilet is still standing strong. Go figure."

"When it comes to renovation, I've seen a lot of weird. Why don't you just use the outhouse for the shower? The long-drop has long been filled in."

"I'm using the outhouse as the basis for the chicken-coup, so it has to be relocated over there. I'd prefer the shower just here."

For the first time he smiled at her, and not in an irritated, condescending way. "I almost wish I could see what you see."

"You will. When it's done."

Mac was calmed by the fact that, in a couple of afternoons, a camp-shower materialised out of recycled iron and beams. Minimal timber needed to be purchased. Dan stayed a post and hung the old door, adding shelves and a bench. He dug some ditches to drain the water away, used old pallets to raise the floor on a bed of coarse river stone gravel, and over laid rubber mats to prevent splinters traumatizing delicate toes. In actual fact – it was the Ritz. Any camper would have been proud.

He showed her how to hitch up the solar heated shower bladders with his simple pulley system. "Looks like you've had your last Servo-shower. Welcome home."

She grunted. She couldn't wait to have a real shower with ceramic tiles and flick mixer hot water. Given that her exchange cubicle would not be here for another century, this was a compromise that she was surprised to admit was not too humiliating. This was so much better than the roadhouse. She had containers of water filled up at the servo. She was going to either be on good terms with Snooks or mortal enemies.

Delivery for her temporary water storage again had a time lag, as did the plumber to install the pump on the bore. Would she ever get used to not being able to have something delivered within hours? Up till now, two or three days had been the ultimate test in her patience! Here they consistently talked in weeks!

As soon as Dan left, she ran for her towel, shampoo, and shower-gel, and braced herself for the shower experience. It was an operation in organisation, lining up toiletries, hanging up her towel and allocating a place to fold her worn clothes up out of the dirt. She added a couple of additional hooks to hang up a clean change of clothes. She had never washed her hair staring up at clouds before. It had a primeval feel about it that set her teeth on edge. Just as she finished rinsing her hair a couple of kookaburras started laughing in their raucous, hilarious way. She jumped. "Not funny", mumbled Mac. At least on the up-side, the temperature of the solar-heated bags was textbook, and she managed to get through her ablutions using only one bladder. That was until she dropped her loofah, and it rolled out into the dirt, and she had to hitch up her second bag of water to wash it clean.

By the time she was dressed and emerged towel drying her hair, she was feeling as though she had not just had a shower but had surmounted an event not unlike an equestrian steeplechase. She had climbed mountains, jumped ditches, forded rivers. She felt exhausted! But Mac believed in this project with all her heart. This was something that was just for her.

As she came around to the stairs of the demountable someone stood up. "Good afternoon. Oh, I am sorry. Did I startle you?" A little, grey-haired lady stood there quite unapologetic, in spite of what she said. Mac stared. She recognised the face but couldn't place where from.

There weren't that many people in Gumleigh. Was she losing it completely? "Have we met?"

"Oh yes. I work at the second-hand op-shop. We did furniture shopping together.   Your donation was very generous. Thank you. I wanted to welcome you to the neighbourhood a little more personal like."

Mac said nothing. Had she come out here to secure another donation?

The lady didn't seem to notice her silence and continued. "I wondered if you liked home-made cooking? I made a lamb casserole..." A shadow passed across her eyes. "It was my mother's favourite recipe," she added hopefully. "It generally gets good reviews..."

Something in Mac's chest skipped and constricted. "Your mother's recipe?" The lady was so tentative in her offering it caught Mac by surprise. She stared at her.

The lady nodded and her spectacles slipped down her nose. Her face was crinkled from years of weather, or perhaps, worry. She could be sixty, seventy... or maybe not. It was hard to tell. Spritely is what people call active oldies. This lady was 'spritely'. "It's a family favourite. My boys still like it. You may have met them; they have the delivery service."

"Oh? The guys who delivered my furniture – they are yours?" They had looked every bit as old as her. Maybe she was ninety!

"The shop?   Ahh..."   She laughed, a little uncomfortable. "Well, I suppose... I guess I do have a few boys around here. Anyway, I wanted to welcome you to The Gums, properly like."

"Oh yes. Of course. Um... well, as you probably remember, my name is Mac. And ahh, thank you." She reached out and shook her hand, feeling like her Mum was standing behind her, pushing her forward with a grim whisper, telling her not to forget her manners.

"Mac. It is a delight to have you as part of The Gums district, for however long. My name is Iris. I put the casserole on your kitchen bench. Didn't want the ants picking it up and carrying it away."

"Oh. Thanks."

She said it as if it was the most customary thing. Iris smiled bashfully as if she had just been given a thousand accolades. "You're welcome. I do hope you like being here." And she left.

6.

Mac blinked as she watched Iris walk down the road. She had carried that dish all the way out to her place on foot? Amazing. What was more astounding was that this woman had just invited herself into her house. Even if it was a demountable donga, it was her... well, her private space. She looked at the enormous casserole dish on the bench. She'd be eating lamb stew for a month of Sundays... breakfast, lunch, and dinner. She'd have to get a dog to help with leftovers!

A dog. Huh. Mac had never allowed herself to entertain such an idea before. In her fourth-floor apartment a dog was an impossible ambition, but here, for some reason, the notion stayed with her. It might not only be possible, but it could have some seriously positive things going for the idea. It would be comforting when the darkness crept in over the paddocks.

She knew immediately that her dog would be a grey German short-haired pointer. Such an active dog could never be accommodated in the small spaces or confined neighbourhoods she was used to. The other thing she knew without consciously thinking about it was the dog's name: Frank-L. The spaces of Frank Lloyd Wright's architecture inspired her. He revolutionised the way she looked at her own landscape, inside and out. Little wonder Utzon could design the iconic Sydney Opera House – he'd been a student in Wright's school. Perhaps this was another way of expressing the idea of opening up the smallness of her life.

She served herself a plate of casserole and unfolded her architectural plans like a tablecloth and sighed as she sat down. It was hard to understand why the discussion about water had caused such a reaction within her. Really, eco-sustainable, organic plans were her bread and butter. It was certainly no insurmountable challenge. It was just... well, it was just another delay... another irritation that contaminated something. But what exactly? It was not really clear what bugged her. Mac always knew her own mind. She was unfamiliar with this feeling of doubt. She stood up and walked around. She had never done so much thinking in her black and white life. It was really awkward. When life was like a set of drawings – dimensioned and planned, things were measured, predictable, safe. No one ever challenged her drawings, except maybe Tommy... and even he would only do so with a fair smattering of respect.

Mac looked outside. The sun was sinking low towards the hills. An old willow tree, gnarled and twisted, stood stoically alone, bent over the remnants of an old fence that ran along a shallow gully towards the back boundary. She hadn't noticed that tree before; really noticed. Suddenly Mac picked up her plate and coffee mug and went outside. She sat facing the silhouette of that bent tree waving its long miserable branches against the flushed evening sky.

Images of her Mum lying on her chaise lounge faded in and out of her vision. "Stanzie," she would say, "there is nothing quite like it... that fresh smell of dew on the grass first thing in the morning... feeling it between your toes. The birds singing so clear at sunset. Have you ever noticed that?" It seemed to soothe her pain-wracked body when she was talking about her childhood. She clucked about her aunt's chooks, and the warm eggs plucked from nests smelling of freshly cut hay. She sighed about the vegie-patch and the sweet-smelling basil and oregano spilling over the edge of the rusty claw-foot bathtub that was the herb garden. Smells. She seemed to remember the smells clearest of all. She'd reminisce about Aunt Lorna's smoky wood stove and the amazing dishes that oven brought forth like a sacred birthing suite. Her mum was a little girl whose rose-coloured glasses never lost their glorious tint.

Hazy and dull, the light faded across the paddocks and went black. She sat still for a long time, playing with her Mum's ring on her right hand, the remainder of the lamb casserole untouched, until the coldness of the dark drove her inside.

❦

"Stanzie! Stanzie!" Mac woke with a jolt and sat up in bed, her damp hair clinging to her neck. She sat there disorientated for a moment. Mum... Mum was calling for her.

She sighed. That was over now. She checked her phone for the time and noticed the dawn light sneaking around the curtains. It didn't seem worthwhile trying to go back to sleep. Mac ran a brush through her hair and pulled on a long cashmere coat. She made a coffee and took her breakfast outside. The last of the winter mornings were cool, and she pulled her feet up underneath the hem of her coat wrapping her fingers around the lip of her coffee cup, steam curling from it in a strange sort of sardonic sneer. Was she going nuts? She sat there, looking at the contorted shapes of that twisted willow-tree again.   Its bare limbs seemed to be waving at her; perhaps reaching out, and she felt a strange connection with its tortured posture. She wondered if that poor tree would ever be free to gracefully stand up tall, or if it was marked forever as a monument to pain. Her pain. She owned that tree now.

Oh.

She had not expected that.

She stared at the wet grass, wondering why she couldn't smell it. Nor did she have an overwhelming desire to feel it between her toes. What was wrong with her? She couldn't even hear any birds. Maybe morning birdsong had been eradicated since Mum was a girl. Or maybe, her Mum's illness made her sentimental... or senile ... and she had lost her bearings of reality. Maybe it never really was how she remembered it. Mac's eyes were grim and held a misty sort of disappointment. She had sincerely believed her mother's ramblings and built a picture of this magnificent sensory haven that was Country. But this place wasn't anything like that. There was no cacophony of singing birds. It was just quiet: vacant. She reached into her pocket and felt around for her ipod. Evidently, she had left it on the bench inside. The effort to retrieve it was too imposing. There was enough noise inside her head to drown out the silence anyway. She had breakfast to finish and her day to begin.

Today she would mark out the front yard. It is the entry-place that sets the tone; the space that is the invitation for the visitors to get away from whatever they had come to retreat from. She saw low hedges, circular gardens, crunching gravel paths and a gentle classical water feature. This is what she understood as 'Retreat'. Perhaps she wanted to generate the feel of a monastery: quiet, still, secluded, away from the turmoil of real life and work deadlines.

She pulled out her tins of fluro spray-paint to print her plan on the ground. This is something she could do independent of the structural work. She went into the hardware shop and bought a brush-cutter from Bob, and then pulled down the last remnants of the front fence. She stacked the old metal gate against a pile of salvaged timbers, the scrolls rusted and warped. What she would do with it she was not sure, but it represented the gateway from the old place to the new. She knew that if she allowed these types of questions to percolate, the ideas would come.

ఞ•ಬಿಲ•ఞ

7.

Late that afternoon, after Dan had left, she sat behind the donga looking again at the knotted profile of the willow tree against the deep tones of the setting sky. She became aware of a distant longing building like a storm far on the horizon. When was the last time she drew a picture? Just a drawing, without the precision of an architectural blueprint? She used to draw what was in her heart, laying it down on paper. She would sketch something for her mum, or her dad, or her teachers, or her neighbours, but mostly it was just to engage in the act of creating. She was no longer ten years old, and somewhere, somehow, that process had transposed to structural dimensions of measurements and space. She had a gift, that's what her teacher had said. Her creativity meant she excelled at this work, but now spontaneity was channelled into the functional and calculated. She craved a type of impulsiveness that didn't have to be purposed, that wasn't driven by outcomes, other than being instinctively imaginative. Was that okay? Was functional the only measure of worth? Could a creative act be worthwhile all by itself? She used to think so. Somewhere, deep within her, that idea resonated with an echo of longing. Did it matter if no one else thought so too? Was such a thing a violation of some silent pragmatic code of modern civilisation... modern women... modern architects?

She remembered her mum framing a sketch she had drawn of their neighbour's geriatric cat. She had hung it so proudly in the hallway. Mum asked Mac to do another and she had been so pleased with how it turned out; much better than the first. Her mum had carefully cut out some cardboard to prevent it bending, and tucked it into a big envelope. She had paid the extra postage to send it off to her dad. As her mum wrote out his last known address, Mac smiled with pride and talked about how pleased Dad would be to get her sketch because he had commented on that cat once. Her mum had nodded enthusiastically. Mac suspected that Mum had probably not believed any of it. She most likely played up his appreciation because she knew it meant so much for Mac to believe it. She wondered how much pride her Mum had to swallow to include her estranged husband in this single act of parenting. Mac sighed. She never heard if Dad got that picture of the cat, or the others. Did he like any of them? Why did it matter so much, not knowing if he ever admired her... artwork? Of course... the artwork. Did he ever acknowledge the hours she painstakingly shaded and toned until she was satisfied? It seemed she was never satisfied though.

Tears welled in her eyes, building like a bubbling crescendo within her chest, begging her to remember. What a gesture! To walk down to the post box with her mother, holding the flap down so Mac could post the cat drawing. It showed Mac more clearly than anything else that her Mum believed... and not just in her art.

Funny how she couldn't actually remember when she stopped drawing. Perhaps it was when she had switched from visual arts to architecture. The urgency to excel and prove her serious professional worth meant she could never have time for a hobby. When her Mum tentatively asked her about her art, she had quickly said she was drawing all the time at work, more than she ever had. That seemed to satisfy her. Mac didn't bother explaining that she mostly used computer software. It was just a different medium anyway. At least, that's what she told herself. There was a physical ache in her arms to hug her mum again, and if she couldn't do that, to hold an art-pad.

஦ଓଔ

The next time Mac walked into town, she bought back a package from the post office. She ripped it open and extracted a box of art pencils, watercolours, pastels, brushes, acrylics, pads of cartridge paper and other supplies. She set everything out on the dining table: instruments clinically arranged, technically prepared, surgically organised, and architecturally aligned. She sat down and took it all in. It felt satisfying to have a space dedicated to this again.

She adjusted her chair. Opened the pad. Held the pencil. And closed her eyes, expecting that urging to rise.

Hmm.

Where was the boiling desire? She waited.

She went to draw. She paused.

She started to make a line, but then stopped. That was how she always commenced a concept design: a single line. This was to be different. No lines that would intersect with angles to become a plan. This was to be her rule: just pain. She wanted to draw her pain.

She sat with her eyes closed, waiting for the images to imprint on the back of her retina like a clearly focused projection screen.

Nothing? Nothing at all.

The pencil snapped in her grip, and she threw the broken bits across the room and stormed outside. She strode across the paddock swiping at her eyes. This was ridiculous! Why was nothing about this what she wanted... or expected? Where was the space, the peace, the retreat? It was like forces swarmed around inside her belly, hounding her, and she could not escape. No matter how fast and how far she walked, they continued to nip at her insides. She knew what she was capable of. She knew who she was. She had felt it a long time ago, but now it was gone, condensing into this thing that would not leave her alone.

She stared up at a silent expanse of clear blue sky, fading in the afternoon light and surrendered to the storm that had crept silently from the distance into her present... and she wondered how long it would bluster within her. She turned and walked back to the donga and sat outside unable to face the thought of casserole again tonight. She sat there, feet on the chair, hugging her knees. The blush red of the horizon created a fascinating silhouette of the willow: rough; symbolic; stylised in its simplicity; potent in its sensuality. This monument was tangible, unattractive, real, yet intriguing in its distortion.

She traced its twisted curves with her eyes... and then impulsively jumped up and grabbed her art-pad, and a fresh pencil from the box. She hunched on the chair outside, pad on her knee and desperately strove to capture this moment in the dying seconds of the day, locking it onto the page. Her hand moved deftly, sketching the twisted, gnarled limbs stretching and straining to escape their tangled pain. Soon their branches would be draped in the mourning garb of its long foliage.

Finally, the light faded, and Mac retreated to her lounge. She propped herself up with cushions and, by the light of her lamp, laid down shadows and form, focused and driven, losing sense of time. And when Mac finally raised her cramped hand and stared at what lay on the page before her, she realised she had drawn her own twisted confusion. Resolutely she laid it aside and declared no one would ever see this journal of her heart. And she cried and cried.

❦ ཨ☙

8.

Most afternoons, Dan came at four o'clock. He didn't chat. He didn't pry. He rarely asked questions. He consulted about the clean-up plan. He gave instructions. He took instructions. They worked hard. He left at six-thirty, sometimes seven. Nothing could have suited Mac more. Progress was being made even with such restricted hours. Digging foundations and pouring concrete would not be too far off her original timeline, and then the construction work proper could start. Mac was smugly confident she had finally found the perfect tradesman. He didn't argue. He didn't spar. If he challenged something he did so with a level of diffidence. He did excellent work. Maybe she could talk him into coming to town to do some other jobs when she moved back. If the weather forecast remained kind, this was going to be completed in record time.

Iris continued to bring food. Mac was certain she had some sort of eating disorder exhibiting symptoms through vicariously feeding other people. There was chicken casserole; beef stew; vegetable bake; shepherd's pie. And not single serves, but enough to feed a family of eight. After a few weeks of evening meals, Mac was well and truly overwhelmed by the invasion of calories. She didn't know how to... well, stem the flood. Mac started feeding Dan copious amounts of food to try and get rid of it without having to say anything disparaging about her love offerings.

56

Dan willingly took a plate. Said it saved him from having to eat when he got home.

She really wanted to handle the food issue with care. Mostly, in the past, she would have sent such a person and their stuff packing. But this was different. She liked Iris. She liked having her visit. She liked the idea that she liked her back.   She liked the idea that she was old and was somebody's mother and grandmother. She liked the idea that Iris wanted to care for her.

"Wouldn't worry about it," Dan said obligingly. "She pretty much does this for all the newcomers." He tucked into another serve. "Beef is my favourite."

She stared at him. "She does this for everyone?" She shook her head in bewilderment at the twang of disappointment in her chest as she realised this was just an obliging routine of rural hospitality. "How long before the initiation is over then?" He laughed at her. "We don't get that many newcomers to Gumleigh so I don't rightly know. She means well. You could just ask her to stop. Never known her to intentionally go against someone's wishes."

"Oh, I couldn't do that. She is being so nice. It's just that there is so much food. I've filled up my freezer to capacity as it is."

"Guess you're okay then. I'll eat here and not at home. Problem solved."

She sighed. It wasn't solved at all. "Could you ask her to stop?"

"Stop what?"

"Well, bringing over food…"

He looked over his fork loaded with casserole and grinned. "Don't think you understand I'm on a good thing here. I don't have to wash up at home when I eat here."

"Dan! Come on. I don't want to hurt her feelings."

"But you're okay if I do?"

"How could you hurt her feelings? You're a local. Doesn't that give you some sort of privilege?"

He shrugged, his grin broadening. "Being local? None that I know of…"

She was annoyed. Why wouldn't he do such a simple thing? "I thought we had an understanding! We've been working together for weeks now!"

Dan looked up and sort of swallowed. His eyes crinkled with amusement. "Oh, I think we understand each other pretty well actually."

"Then do this. Please?"

"Do… what exactly?"

"Ask Iris to give up bringing all that food…"

"I'm not paid to be your messenger boy."

"No! You're not! I thought you might do it because you are a friend! Why is that so much to ask?"

He put down his fork and paused for a moment. Mac turned away and smiled to herself and waited. She had him in the palm of her hand. She knew it.

"Well, if this is what you call friendship, I'm kind of not flattered. Pretty shallow sort of affair. Business associates certainly; neighbours, I'd even pay that. But friends? Not even close. Guess I'll just go back to doing the washing-up at home. But thanks for the offer just the same." He took his plate over to the kitchen bench and walked out. She heard his ute drive away a minute later.

The silence was loud. Very loud. She had no idea what just happened. She looked at his unfinished meal in stunned disbelief. Really? She had been micro-seconds away from getting him to do a simple favour and somehow it had instantly turned on its head. It confused her. Pompous, ignorant, thoughtless individual! Of course, they were friends. They worked well together. They didn't fight. What was that if it was not friendship?

␿€ɢɤ

Mac tossed all night. Where on earth would she get another builder in a place such as Gumleigh? She Googled a few options; emailed a couple of contacts at Blackstone. She consoled herself that if she fought for her contract he'd have to stay, but she doubted that a cranky, legally bound tradesman maliciously sabotaging her dream-project was an outcome she should fight for. He could wreck her. She cursed Dan Henry, she cursed Iris and she cursed the beef stew! It was unbelievably inconvenient!

That next afternoon Dan rocked up in his work-duds and jumped out of his ute. Mac stared at him in disbelief. "You're here?"

"Yeah." He checked his phone. "It's after four."

"Well, after yesterday I thought..." She blinked. He was obviously ready to work.

"Didn't think you sacked me. We have a contract." Mac inhaled quickly. He would push to enforce their contract? That was her line! "The way you left! I wasn't sure you would show up this afternoon."

He just looked at her. "You don't want me to continue?" In one joyful moment he wondered if this was his out.

"You're the one who walked out in a huff like some prepubescent teenager."

"My point was I would rather wash up the dishes at home, - a job, by the way, that I loathe - in preference to the strings-attached arrangement you seem to think is called friendship."

"Well, I obviously got that wrong! I thought you liked Iris's cooking."

"Yep, I do. And the point is...?"

"So... well... I just thought..."

"You just thought it would be to my advantage to say the awkward things you don't want to?"

"I was thinking more that it would be easier to tell someone whom you already know that I am only one person, and the amounts are ridiculously large."

"You don't give up easily do you?"

"Give up? I don't have to. I am right. How can you think that is using you?"

"Bingo. Because it is."

"Huh!! What is your problem? Can't friends ask favours from each other?"

"Friends? Sure." It didn't seem like he would say anything more, but then he suddenly added, "You know our arrangement stands and falls on the dotted line... and as such is purely professional. So, I apologise if accepting your food confused that understanding."

"You're nuts! We aren't sleeping together. It is just left-over beef stew."

"Which makes it all the more... weird!" Mac glared at him. "It is just stew!"

"So, tell her you don't want it. Mac, just do it. 'Easy' isn't what matters here. I would have thought you were no stranger to something a little uncomfortable."

She faltered. Uncomfortable? Actually, she was pretty familiar with that. Why would it bother her what Iris thought? A string of past relationships flashed before her eyes in a kind of death-bed clarity. Truth had killed each one. "I don't want to offend her that's all."

"My goodness this is cracked! She's more likely to be disappointed that you can't tell her what you really want."

"Do you think so? I really like her popping in. She's been a friend... and in a place like this, making friends isn't easy," she said pointedly.

At that he smirked and strapped on his tool-belt as he walked over to the building site. "Actually, I thought it wasn't too hard – bring a casserole or sign a contract: you're good."

She scowled and turned her back, tears stinging the backs of her eyes. How dare he be so unkind? He had no idea about her life. She had thought he was different. She had thought he was... well, friendly. That, it seems, is a rare commodity. Who did she know who hadn't dropped her like a hot frying pan once things got uncomfortable? She couldn't think of anyone. Well, maybe Tommy.

Uncomfortable.   The reality of her life was bleaker than she ever imagined. How was it possible to spend time with people and be so lonely? It was like dying of thirst in the middle of the ocean. Water, water everywhere and not a drop to drink. She wondered for a moment if dying on the inside was this type of uncomfortable.

Damn Dan Henry. He had no idea!

❧ ❧

9.

Iris tapped on the door of the demountable juggling a casserole dish. It smelt wonderful... reminiscent of a country kitchen that wafted into the recesses of Mac's memory. She sat down at the table and Mac pressed the button on the electric jug. She took a deep breath. This could be the last cup of coffee with Iris like this. Mac resolved to savour the moment and have the coffee first. Then she could break the news, and maybe her friendship.

"Want to sit outside? I like it there. Sometimes I sit and watch the sunset." She blushed as if she was disclosing a sin akin to gluttony, or worse even... infidelity. Sitting, doing nothing: it felt shamefully indulgent.

They sat together and looked out over the paddocks. Iris didn't seem scandalised by just sitting in the quiet with a friend, sipping coffee. Somehow it felt a little surreal, as though life as she knew it had never existed before this moment. Friend. This felt like friendship. But perhaps Dan was right. Perhaps it wasn't. She knew she would need to say something, and she was annoyed that Iris couldn't see the obvious – that she didn't feed a crew of workers. How could her emotions change so painfully in so short a time... shame, exhilaration, fear, contentment, annoyance? Nothing was definite. And yet everything felt more real than it had in a long time. It was so confusing.

"You seem quiet, Dear. Is your project coming along okay?"

"Hmmm," she said noncommittally. "I had a bit of an argument with Dan, but I think we're okay now."

"An argument? With Dan. Oh." She raised an eyebrow and her face creased in concern.

"Well. Sort of. I asked him to do something. He refused. So, he left."

"He left? He's not working here anymore?"

"Well, that's the weird thing. He turned up yesterday like nothing had happened. I didn't expect that."

Iris said nothing but quietly drank her cup of tea. She looked at the tree that framed their vision, deep in thought.

Mac sighed. Okay. It was now. "Iris...?" Iris sat very still. "Iris... I... well, I wanted to thank you for visiting. And for the food. It has been wonderful not to have to cook. I haven't had someone cook for me since... since forever.

When mum's treatment got too much I was cooking and caring for her and working full-time. It was exhausting. And then after the funeral... well I lost the plot a bit there. All the emotional and physical pressure started coming out in unusual ways. I'd phase out... or find myself doing stuff I didn't realise I was doing. The doctor said it was stress induced amnesia... not really severe, but enough to cause concern. One time I woke up and found I had been packing up the unit at night. They didn't think it was sleep walking – as it normally is... but along those lines. My doctor said I should take some leave. That's why I came here. It was important that I have a break. It's just… well…" She stopped. How does she say it?

"Well, it has been my pleasure. It seems plenty of people still like home cooked meals, even these days. You sound hesitant though?"

Mac grimaced and stared at her mug. Dan was right. This was nuts. She plunged in. "It's just that I don't eat that much food. I might have to get a dog to get through it. I really like you coming though. I was giving meals to Dan… but now that we've had that fight, he's decided he'd prefer chores at home than eating with me… so, I'm stuck. I just wanted to ask if you could not bring food? Please…?" she finished lamely.

"You want me to stop bringing you meals… altogether, or just not so much?"

Mac nodded apologetically. "Maybe in another year. I have enough to feed the entire nation of India in my freezer at the moment."

"But it's okay if I come to visit… for a coffee maybe?"

"Really? I would love that!"

Iris burst out laughing. A relaxed sort of bubbling that just seem to make her crinkled face shine.

Mac looked up stunned, the contagious effect of her delight spreading into her eyes. "What's so funny?"

"You looked so serious I thought it was going to be something quite awful. I always cook; always have. I find it breaks down barriers to offer people meals. I haven't had many times where it has created one though. Although now I think about it, not many singles come to a place like Gumleigh. Families mainly. Guess that's it..."

Mac smiled. "You're not offended?"

"Of course, Dear. Massively offended. I've been cooking since I was five and this is the first time anyone has asked me to stop. This will cost you many cups of tea. I hope you realise that."

Mac let out a deep sigh. How could she have been so terrified?

Iris looked up, her smile fading. "Since we're giving out confessions. I have one of my own. But I fear that maybe you may not think it as benign as over feeding you."

Mac looked out at the tree. She wondered in a relaxed sort of way what terrible thing this sweet little lady could say that would change anything.

"You know Gumleigh is a small community, and everyone pretty much knows everyone. There are lots of connections. Like... I grew up here."

"I figured that..." Mac's voice faded out. Although Dan did say 'local' didn't provide any sort of privilege. She didn't believe that. Local was code for "in" and she knew she was still "out". Iris looked at Mac, and her crinkles smiled. It encouraged Mac to offer the thought out loud.

"I thought in country places, local connections gave a sort of credibility. And I confess I wanted Dan to talk to you about the food. But he wouldn't."

"He mentioned that..."

"What? He made this big song and dance about not being my messenger boy and said my idea of friendship was shallow and mercenary, and then stormed out. But he told you anyway? The man is psycho."

Iris paused, staring at the tree through her glasses. She was not too worried. She had an inkling about what was going on: a hope really. "Well, "local" is sort of what I wanted to talk to you about. I grew up here."

"Hmm. You said that."

"What I'm trying to say is... really local. When I say I grew up here, I mean here, in this house... your house. It occurred to me that you may not realise this cottage belonged to our family. My maiden name was Guthrie."

Mac put down her cup and swore under her breath. "Guthrie's Road? No way! You've been bringing me food, so you could keep tabs on what I'm doing to your house?" Did it have anything to do with her... all those casseroles?

"Well, it's been vacant for years. We had to wait for certain details to be finalised from Dave's death... and then the subdivision process took a while. It's been on the market for a long time. No one seemed terribly interested in the block. It's always been a rocky barren sort of knoll, except for along the creek. And Gumleigh is an out of the way sort of place. When my parents built the new house where we live now, I was only a young thing, and it was such an adventure. My parents rented this out until the maintenance was more than what they could get for it. Then Dave and I lived in in this little cottage for years after we were married. It was so run down back then, and Dave worked hard on it. The boys went to school here... caught the bus up on the road. Oh, I admit, I have been very curious. Dan says the plans you have are quite stunning."

"Dan said that?"

"Oh yes. I would say he is quite the fan."

"Dan Henry? A fan. There's a new idea."

"I would like to see your plans sometime... unless of course, they are designated secret until it all comes together? Dan wouldn't show them to me of course. He says they are not his to share."

She thought of the times she had rifled over other people's designs with Tommy, pulling them apart and taking worthwhile ideas as their own. She would never take a whole plan and steal it, but she'd swapped components like a well-used lego box. "You do know my studio will not look anything like it used to?"

"I'm delighted that someone is loving this place again... in new ways. I'm expecting it to be unexpected."

"My designs are... different. This is no exception. Perhaps more so. It could destroy every memory you have of growing up here."

Iris sat looking at the willow-tree. That tree held many of her own secrets – like a sage old wise-woman. "You're worried that the way you build your house could overtake my memories? That's a curious thought." She went quiet, silently contemplating the question that sat between them. She seemed to say nothing forever. Mac braced herself. Finally, Iris sighed gently. "I wonder if the reverse is also true. What if the memories I hold change the way you look at your project?"

Now Mac cringed. How could anything Iris say deconstruct her view of what she saw? Nah. She dismissed it. How could it change what was already mapped? It wouldn't... couldn't. She was a person who knew her own mind, and her mind was set.

"Could I share something with you?" Iris asked eventually. "It is quite personal..."

Mac held her breath, willing herself not to move. What bothered her was not whether this might or could change anything. Mac just didn't know if she had any reserves to hold other people's personal stuff. Did she want to risk that? She looked over at Iris's mild face in the evening light and didn't think that her stuff could possibly be that threatening. It gave her courage. She shrugged then. "Sure," she said, and then added respectfully. "If you would like to."

Iris stood and started to stack up the cups on the tray. "I would like to; very much. I promise I will bring it over when it is ready. Is that okay?"

Mac raised her eyebrows in a fine arch. She had kind of expected a tirade of mushy, homely stories: memories like chopping wood and getting splinters in her fingers... or cinnamon apple tea-scrolls smelling divine as they were taken from the smoky combustion wood stove. Much like another version of her mum's inexhaustible store of recollections of Aunt Lorna's place. That was what her mum's generation did: reminisce through rose coloured glasses. "Sure. When you are ready," she said, and as she spoke, suddenly she was anticipating a beautiful surprise.

10.

Mac got up early and drove along the motorway. She turned the music up, put the top of her convertible down and allowed herself to enjoy the drive. The email she had been waiting for had come through. If the promise of Iris's gift was like anticipating a birthday, this was like Christmas. It felt strange to be doing this, not because she had to, or needed to, but just because she could. No timetables, no schedules, no pressure... just her own agenda. And dare she admit it – it was just a tad frivolous because it was not pragmatically driven.

She checked the address on her phone and pulled up beside the gutter. The house was an unassuming suburban double-storey with lots of concrete as driveway. Dated decades ago. It spoke of boring, normal, usual, conformity, not standing out. It made Mac cringe and then she reprimanded herself. She shouldn't judge people's lives by their houses. She was not here to design or remodel or renovate. She was here for something completely not work.

She knocked on the door. A long gangly woman answered and gave her a wonderful toothy smile, ushering her inside. They went through the dark corridor to a large downstairs room. A rush of half a dozen puppies greeted her. The dusky mother dog was lying contented and exhausted in the corner. Mac giggled nervously as she looked around at all this energy, speculating which would be her Frank-L. She

71

wondered if she was the kind of pet-buyer who would insist on taking the boldest, most dominating and rambunctious puppy in the litter; or be attracted to the whining, weak runt sulking in the corner? She shrugged. She had no idea, even though she had read all the recommendations. She looked helplessly at the lady who presided over the litter with matriarchal pride.

"You asked very specifically for dark grey colouring. All our puppies are healthy and have good temperament traits," she said through that toothy smile. Mac wondered if her glorious leer hid Cruella de Vil tendencies. This was a little overwhelming. She knew there were some very definite technical things to look for and felt her single request of a particular colour reeked of inexperience, incompetence, naivety. The woman just stood there grinning, implying that any of her puppies would be a good option when starting on the adventure of canine ownership.

Finally, the woman stepped forward, picking up a grey sweetie. "Actually, all our puppies are pre-sold, and many have already gone to their homes, so this is your allocated pup. Here he is." Well, why didn't she say so? Mac looked at him, cute and adorable, and felt herself flinch. She hadn't thought about what a puppy would be like. She had only pictured herself with a dog, not a tiny, dependent, whimpering, barking, mischievous, playful baby. It seemed too much. Mac stared wide-eyed as the woman held him out to her.

The woman frowned then.   She was obviously disturbed that Mac did not enthusiastically gush forward, affectionately eager to embrace her progeny. "Oh. Well." She coughed and cleared her throat.   "Ahh, I wouldn't normally suggest this," she said as she warily eyed her reluctant customer, and snuggled the puppy close to her bosom, "but I wonder if a mature dog would be more to your liking?" and she put the puppy back on the floor, shooing it protectively towards the others. "I have a retired bitch – she's been de-sexed since weening her last litter. She's..." The woman cleared her throat emotionally, "Well, it wouldn't be right for her to whelp again. She's been an excellent mother. We are looking for a suitable companion for her retirement. Would you like to meet her? She's a beautiful, dappled grey..." she added as if this offer would therefore culminate in a foregone conclusion. Mac raised her brows. It sounded like the dog was buying her, and it was Mac's privilege to spend the money to secure the honour to be her companion. Dog owners were weird.

Mac looked into those dark brown eyes and fell in love. Frank-L was going to be a girl-name after all. She wondered if there were important rules about changing doggy-names by deed pol. It could be a new name to represent her new life, now that she was a retired professional: like a nun entering an Abbey; or an actress relinquishing her stage name. She couldn't help it. Another metaphor came unheeded. In a way it did feel like she was rescuing her from the streets. Her working days were over.

∞※∞

Frank-L settled into Mac's donga with matriarchal ease. Mac felt sure that if a dog could cook, Frank-L would have presided over mashed-potato and casseroles with more authority than Iris. She smiled to herself and was a little grateful she already had a fridge full of food, so she didn't have to test who was going to win that territorial battle. Perhaps the gangly dog-lady had left her mark.

Frank-L was indeed devoted company. It was so refreshing, thinking about her world with another soul in it... and trying to figure out how it was going to work. Mac had never needed to do that. Well, not until her Mum became sick. She had resented rearranging her life because her Mum needed her. She had been so impatient to get back on track; get on with only ever having to look after herself and her clients. But actually, she realised it wasn't like that at all. She had not suspended her life to care; it had been a remarkable season in her relationship with her mother that was over too soon. Way too soon. She had not expected this cavernous hole, a hole that was missing her mum like crazy. It had changed something in her. She wanted to fill it with more than... well, she just wanted more.

That evening, as she rubbed Frank-L's ears and ate casserole, and looked out over the paddocks, Mac sketched a fun cartoon of Frank-L. She was wearing an apron, cooking in the kitchen... but not practical meatloaf and vegies for a thousand puppies, like the proverbial woman who lived in a shoe. Instead, she was decorating a black-forest torte with loads of cherries and whipped cream; an extravagant freedom to expand her horizons and do something just for her.

11.

No matter how many times Mac experienced the ritual of pouring footings, she always anticipated that heart-in-the-mouth, this-is-the-laying-foundations moment. She believed she would never get bored with it. She would order champagne, bring a cheese and fruit platter, then she would sit in the shade of the rubbish skip on a picnic rug with her clients and watch it take form. Her colleagues teased her about making so much of one frivolous moment within a whole project time-line. Yet she insisted they celebrate the adventure of fulfilling a dream, demanding they savour the moments they had invested in. She always invited her clients to take part in it, and in the end, she was the architectural consultant they asked to manage their projects again and again. Of course, if the client scorned the idea of relishing this dream-defining-moment, she would allow herself the extravagance of a Snickers bar and a diet coke.

And now, this was the first time this ritual would be celebrating her dream being grounded. It seemed that it warranted more than a Snickers and a coke, but then Champagne, with a cheese and fruit platter seemed a little out of place by yourself. She thought she would ask Iris to share her picnic-rug moment. And she'd add an extra glass for Dan, just in case. She wondered if that was just a little bit tragic: an old woman and a paid contractor.

Mac moved the outside table and chairs so they sat in full view of the pouring, added a white linen cloth, serviettes and the platter for her Champagne breakfast. She put a special treat in Frank-L's bowl beside her chair and waited in anticipation of the day's proceedings. Dan pulled up in his ute with Iris as his passenger, just as the morning light was shining through the trees that lined the road. Iris smiled and gave her a wave as he opened the door for her, and Frank-L bounded over expectantly waiting for Dan to rub her ears. Mac felt a lump in her throat as she watched them laugh good-naturedly. It had the feel of family, and she wondered with a knot of panic if Christmas was going to be too hard this year. Perhaps she could skip it.

Iris sat with graceful ease looking with delight at the fluted glasses and small plates, and her selection of delicacies. Dan stood back and punched in something on his phone while he checked the time that the truck and crew were to arrive. Mac came over and nudged him, offering him a glass. He stared at it, and then at Mac. He shook his head in a kind of disbelieving stupor. "You really were serious? You're all set up like you're getting married."

She laughed at that and nodded slowly. "Yes, I guess you're right. This is a dream, a long time in the planning. The beginning of a beautiful mortgage together."

He looked into her eyes and then turned away. "Well, since I am an invited guest... but I'll have a coke. I am on the job." He came over and straddled his chair in a self-conscious, not-sure-how-to-do-this sort of way. Mac looked over the site, prepped and waiting, the morning mist shrouding it in a little bit of mystery. Perhaps she should have left Dan out of it altogether. It was meant to be special, and he was downgrading her moment by his awkwardness.

She remembered different clients and their varied responses to her invitation: the excitement, the nervous giggles, the worried, anxious looks, protectively presiding over their site, and she had always been there to allay their fears and to soothe their worries and to encourage them to enjoy the exhilaration of seeing their dream materialise. No one was there to do this for her. Just once she wanted someone to do something like that for her. Mac went inside and grabbed Dan a coke, and as she sat it down on the table her phone rang. She quickly excused herself and turned away as she answered, "Oh? Yes, this is Constance Macintosh. No, of course not... I've had no contact..." and she walked away out of hearing.

She hung up and was putting her phone back in her jean's pocket as she returned to the table with the slightest frown on her brow. Dan passed the platter to Iris and raised his eyebrows. The Champagne was untouched in its glass, and he sat on the chair rather than straddling it. Coke in hand, he tucked into some of the fruit. He looked at her with a broadening grin as he waved some cheese and cracker biscuits with approval. "Unbelievable!"

"I know! Who calls at this hour?"

"I was thinking more that your name is Constance, and you go by Mac. How is that possible?"

"What do you mean? I can go by whatever I want."

"Sure... but Constance, that is stunning. It suits you. Constance..." he said, savouring the sound as he considered a strawberry. "Why would you be ashamed of a name like that?" And he popped the fruit in his mouth.

She blinked and said nothing. Did he say stunning? Never in all her life did she think of her name as beautiful. She was sure he was going to add to the string of snide comments and embarrassing giggles. It was old-fashioned and awkward; much like Dan sitting in his jeans and leather belt by her white linen cloth refusing to hold a Champagne flute. It didn't seem to fit. She swallowed and said quietly, "My mother always told me that. But here I go by Mac." As she turned away, she blinked back emotion that struggled to stay down and was relieved to see the truck rolling up the road. "The concreters are here," she snapped, "Finally!"

❧ ഇⰃ❧

The banter of concreters and the hum of the mixer created a kind of blue-collar white noise that went unnoticed as she watched, with an almost out-of-body quality, what was happening. She constructed her retreat again in her mind: the long, large windows; the blend of contemporary and classic country; the curves of the garden; the ageless stone-walls merging into the modern lines of the facade.

Dan's smiling eyes echoed around in her head, *"Constance, that suits you..."* What right did he have to say that? She should have been more guarded, but that phone-call had taken her by surprise. Now she was walking around, off centre, trying to look like nothing was unsettling. But it was. How many people even knew her as Constance? She could barely account for half a dozen individuals on the planet.

She sat in the receding shade as the morning sun rose, snapping photos on her phone of the foundations being poured, and snorted. She took another photo, as the next concrete truck rolled up and the men hollered out their directions like waving an airliner into dock. They were wading around in their gumboots, shovelling the grey concrete-slurry spilling out over the footings. It felt weird to have someone other than her Mum say that Constance suited her. Stunning? She hardly thought so. She had always told herself that if she couldn't be beautiful, she could get things done. 'Doing' was what she was good at. Just like Dad.

ᔐᵒᔑᏯᏳ

12.

Mac insisted that the slab have premium curing time. Dan accommodated that by focusing on finishing his renovating job at the motel. They agreed that he would start working full time on her site when he was done. She found the space to work alone on the garden much easier than she thought. It reminded her of that saying... "Life is a journey, not a destination". She had no idea where she had heard that. Maybe it was the Dalai Lama... or some medieval saint. Maybe it was Mum; she had often said things like that. Mac had considered it a vague, directionless, lost sort of idea. But now it fitted. She was working on being found, on finding home and going there. Or at least getting closer. And that was as much about the journey part, as the ending.

She created her own metaphor. This studio retreat was a study in light and shade like the classic art-masters. It was the colour and tone on the canvas, not the frame it stood in that was the real masterpiece. That was her hope above hope: that the act of putting paint on canvas would recreate something in her. Or maybe create something totally new.

Mac thought about going back and touching base with Tomlin while the slab was curing, but she knew he would give her work. Of course, he would. She would even ask for it. No, she was going to stay away and continue landscaping, creating garden beds and retaining walls... the peripheral places that would not impede direct access to the site. She was focused on the front yard and each day she could see another part of the whole emerging.

It was a quiet couple of weeks. Even Iris said she was working longer hours at the shop while one of her main-stay volunteers went to visit family out west. The physical work and her tired body muted Mac's thoughts. It was strange to her that the dust and the grime felt like clean work. Fresh air and soil; wheelbarrow and hoe. It was... well... organic.

Back to basics. She ended up cancelling the portable shower suite. It saved her the hire money. If she could survive the chill of early mornings, then when the warmer weather established, it would not be necessary. At least that is what she told herself... these were the safer rationales. She felt uncomfortable admitting she enjoyed the freedom of washing her hair looking at clouds floating past with trees swaying in the fringes of her vision. Nothing to hide behind. For an artist who did her stint of nude portraits, Mac decided she was a bit of a prude.

In among the hours of shovelling topsoil into garden-beds and raking and seeding lawn, Mac could hear that voice, that thin and hollow voice on the phone. He sounded like he could have just been reading from a newspaper. So impersonal. "I'm looking for Constance Macintosh – daughter of Donny and Shirley Macintosh."

"Yes, this is Constance Macintosh..." Oh boy. That was personal.

One rainy afternoon, Mac sat with her collection of magazines and samples that had been gradually growing... like her garden. She played with the colour and design of her rooms. She had only randomly dabbled with interior design before because Tommy considered it a specialist arena that was not to be trespassed. Why would you ask an electrician to do your plumbing? But this was her project – and she could do whatever she wanted. It felt a little rebellious to insist that she would take control of this.

When the rain cleared, she took Frank-L for a drive to collect her mail. There were a number of parcels of samples and supplies she had ordered. She came down the Post Office stairs juggling her deliveries and tried to untie Frank-L from the lamppost. A kid spotted her and came over; he helpfully grabbed Frank-L's lead for her.

"Hey. Like ya dog," he said without ceremony. Mac smiled. "Thanks. I like her too."

"She looks kinda old though. Going grey."

"Hmm. I guess I never thought about that. The lady who sold her to me said it was a 'nice dappled' colour. Do you think she might have been putting me on? Poor thing might just be old." And she reached down and rubbed Frank-L's ears.

He laughed so the freckles across his nose crinkled. "What's her name then?"

"I call her Frank-L."

"Like ankle?" he asked waving his foot at her. "Frankle, Frankle, bite my ankle!"

She laughed. She had never had much to do with kids. She liked his engaging way... without the cheeky-smart attitude she would have expected. "Yep – exactly."

"Huh. That's stupid. It's not even a real name."

"It is, sort of. I named her after a very famous architect, Frank Lloyd Wright. That is very long, so I shortened it to Frank-L. L for Lloyd." Most people assumed she was named after Viktor Frankl, although Mac was not too ashamed to have a twofold namesake, especially if it was a man who survived German concentration camps and helped people find meaning in their pain. That worked for her too.

The boy shrugged, unimpressed. "I've got a scooter. I could show you sometime..."

Mac smiled; a bit uncomfortable by his unabashed invitation. "You should probably go home now..."

"What's your name?" he persisted.

"Um... Well, you might not think it's a real name..."

"Huh. My friend's name is Gull. That's not a real name either. That's a bird. But he's my friend."

"My Mum called me Stanzie."

"Not so bad really. You could be called Budgie. That's what I tell Gull."

Mac laughed. "So, what's your name? Since we are exchanging state secrets..."

"Todd."

"Well Todd, thank you for your help. It was very kind."

"Sure Miss Stanzie? Yeah, that is kinda weird. But hey: I like you."

Mac smiled. His unaffected honesty made her feel more like Stanzie than she had felt for a long time. She started walking to the car. "It was lovely to meet you, Todd. I have to get Frank-L home now," and she jolted as she realised what she had said. Home.

Mac swiped at her forehead and took a long drink from her water bottle. She had finished slashing back the long yellow grass that had matted along the side fence. She made her lunch and found herself sitting on the coolness of her concrete slab, in the shade of the old stone wall, slowly crunching her apple. She sat looking out over the back paddocks and the willow tree. Again.

What was it about that ugly thing that was so fascinating? It was truly grotesque, so different from the tidy, soothing, welcoming gardens that she had created in her sketchbook for the front entry: neat and clean and proportioned; predictable and symmetrical and tame. This tree was everything her concept was not. It was unruly, desolate,   asymmetrical,   contorted,   irregular,   and unpredictable.

She turned the pages in her visual-diary and looked back over some of her willow tree drawings. Dark clouds hovered in many of them. The contrast was palpable and stark. And just as she had unearthed an urging to hold an art pencil, there was a storm brewing inside of her to work out how to make this fit. If she was trying to make sense of her life, this tree had to fit. She wanted so much to believe it could, it would. She just had to find out how.

She threw away her apple core and called Frank-L. They walked down to the tree and wandered around it, Frank-L sniffing and scratching with anticipation of a great find. She reached out and traced the lines of the knotted trunk. There was a wild part of her... an ugly, tormented part... that didn't fit either. How could she make space for something that was so disagreeable? Why didn't she just hire a contractor and bulldoze it? She had done that to desolate, ugly, twisted things before. Just pretend that it was never there. But Mac could no more ignore this, or hide it, or shun it... than stop breathing. Now she needed to... damn it, she absolutely had to accommodate it... even feature it. It was an undeniable part of this place... its history, its present. She sat on her haunches under its bare branches and closed her eyes. She could feel the wind through its lonely, feebly dressed limbs. How incredibly sad she felt inside. How exposed. Naked. Frank-L sat beside her quietly, and she became aware that in this silence the limbs of the willow were embracing her in a reverent moment.

Mac walked back to the demountable and grabbed the brush-cutter. She went back and furiously attacked the long grass that tangled up around the trunk, drowning out the silence in the wild whirl of noise and dust. Frank-L wandered the paddock, rambling in the freedom of empty space with no fences, barking at grasshoppers as they whirred away on the breeze. And when she returned, Frank-L lay in the shade of the trunk, panting and embarrassed by her juvenile frivolous escapades.

Mac was so absorbed in clearing the tangle that years of accumulated weeds had created, and avoiding rocks, that she didn't see Dan stroll over. Mac jolted when she looked up, and quickly turned off the motor.

"Didn't mean to disturb you," he said with a shrug. "How long have you been there?" she asked tracking in her mind if she had swiped any tears that seemed to flow unbidden at mysterious times without any rhyme or rhythm.

"Hmm? Not long." It didn't mean anything.

"I thought you said you had work at least until the eighteenth. We agreed that we wouldn't start again until then."

"Yeah. We did." He squatted down by Frank-L, rubbing her satin grey ears.

"Then go away. I'm not paying you to pat my dog." She faltered when he stood up and raised his hands, like he was under siege. "Not everything is on the clock. Just thought I'd see if you needed anything... gratis."

Mac blushed silently as she admitted to herself that she accounted for every little service rendered to clients in her invoices. She expected the same from everyone else. But here Dan was offering something for nothing. Was there a catch? Since he asked, what did she need? In truth she didn't know. A shoulder to cry on? Dan Henry hardly looked like the type for that. She shook her head. "Nope. Can't think of anything. Pretty good thank you."

He paused and went to say something and then stopped. "Okay. Well. Guess coming here after four has become a bit of a habit. It only takes twenty-one days to form a new habit they say..."

She shrugged awkwardly. Who would have thought that she would become somebody's bad habit? "Well thanks for popping by. But like I said, pretty sorted."

He stood up tall and acknowledged it for what it was: a shut down. He nodded. "Fair enough..."

"I'll see you on the eighteenth then?"

"I'll call in tomorrow. Just to see how things are."

"Oh. Well then. I'll see if I can be a little more respectable for visitors," she said indicating her dirty, grass stained jeans.

He grinned. "Don't bother. I'm not expecting you to entertain me. I just want to satisfy myself that you're doing all right. See you tomorrow." And he left.

She stood looking at him walk away. Was he trying to be friendly? But he had said that he didn't want her friendship. Did he think she needed babysitting? She'd done life solo for so long now she was pretty good at it. Did he have some altruistic sense of responsibility? No money or business in that. She didn't get it. The man was an enigma, a puzzle that required too much thought and energy just now. She shrugged and restarted the motor and went back to slashing the weeds with frenetic intensity.

13

Mac stood looking at the single standard removalist carton sitting in the middle of her lounge. This was it? This was the sum of the life of the man: Donald Dennis Macintosh. Donny. D-D. She couldn't breathe. She couldn't move. She couldn't open it. Why was she surprised? Why did she expect more?   Not more stuff necessarily, but more like... significance. Was this what sixty years of 'Doing' came to? One cardboard box?

The irony that her dad had not long out-lived his wife was screaming at her. That first phone call had been followed by a number of others. Next of kin. She hadn't even been notified of the funeral. His landlady had sent this box to her. Now Mac was not sure she wanted to know. But here it was. In truth, she just wanted to dump it. Oh, she wanted to. But she also wondered if she would always wonder; and wondered if the wondering would be a greater heartache than just knowing the simple, ugly truth.

If it had not been that hard to find her – if a landlady could do it – why? Why had there been twenty-two years of silence? Why? He might have known where she was, or at least worked out how to find where she was; that was so unfair. Was she not clever enough, or pretty enough, or smart enough? What did it take to be the daughter that he wanted? Mum had been pretty and talented and kind. That wasn't enough either. Mac had so wanted to defend his search for satisfaction and blame it on some flaw that, if corrected, might have kept him home. But as she stared at this box: this plain, unimpressive, pathetic carton, she wondered where the flaw really lay. Perhaps it wasn't her fault, or her Mum's. Perhaps it represented its owner: plain, unimpressive, pathetic. She swallowed and turned away. How could she be so disloyal after all these years of defending him?

Mum, in all her giftedness had ended up teaching students in their living room at the ordinary little piano in the corner. But she never seemed to resent the lack of musical accomplishment that those around her had acclaimed was her destiny. She always had a smile for her pupils, and they loved the way she opened the world of music to them through the window of her heart. Many of her past students had come to her funeral: one had accompanied Mum's favourite hymn; another played an original composition that Shirley had written herself many years ago. There was something profoundly beautiful and meaningful in the way she had invested in the art she loved and imparted it to others. They loved her for it.

Mac turned back and stared at the carton. What did he love? Mum said he had been an artist who painted with incredible majesty and power. She had fallen in love with that passionate artist. But somewhere in the years that ensured, the artist receded and remained hidden in a shadow. His passion became fury. Mac closed her eyes and saw herself climbing under the covers at night shutting her ears to the shouts and the crashes in the living room. How could she not remember that? Her mother bore the brunt of that frustrated ferocity. She saw her eight-year-old desolate, unreasoned rage lashing out at her mother after he left. How dare her mother send him away! Those weeks after her birthday were full of wild, unrestrained tears… for both of them. Life would never be normal again. Her mother immersed herself in music like a woman who had been dying of thirst. For her eighth birthday her mum gave her paints and art lessons. She told her it was a gift from Dad before he left, a going away present: artist to artist. That was the only reason Mac had taken much interest in it. Dad would be pleased. Mum never changed her story, but now Mac couldn't believe that the owner of one single carton looked like anyone who might be interested in a third grader's art classes. She got up and went down to the tree, and sat up against that unruly twisted trunk, lonely and lost, like that little girl. She huddled there, wishing she had been kinder to her mother; more insightful than her tantrums; and more grown up than her years. But through the tears, she admitted she never was. The tragedy of her childhood was just that: she never was.

⁓ଅଓ⁓

Dan had a slight frown as he walked down to the tree. He stood there watching Mac… Constance… frantically dragging rocks from around it. "Need a hand with any of that?" he asked benignly.

She supressed a quip on her lips and sighed, as if caught out. "Sure. You're obviously not going to stay away, so it is easier if you're doing something. I'm not paying you though."

He shrugged. "So, what's the point here?"

This whole thing was frustrating. "I don't know. This tree is not the type of thing I normally go for. It's ugly; it's twisted and... and... and I hardly know why I'm bothering." She paused awkwardly. She felt so angry that she was even bothering. "But well, it's... interesting." She cringed. She couldn't think of a better word. Perhaps obsession was closer to the truth.

"It's certainly that," he offered noncommittally.

She determinedly pushed at a rock, the sound of her own voice grating her nerves. "I was thinking about making a contemplation place... a sort of thinking space. While the willow is in leaf, it is shrouded and shaded. Now that I've slashed the grass back, I'm also thinking maybe a fishpond, reeds... an arbour... like a gazebo for shade. I could grow a grapevine over it. I thought I might swing the original gate on the old fence post here, and wind a wisteria, or maybe honeysuckle... something old fashioned, along a trestle here. I don't know... it all sort of fits with the Retreat idea."

He smiled at that... and said nothing.

"What?" she said. "The guru is tentatively exploring the uncertain. It seems like unfamiliar territory..."

"Rubbish. There is nothing tentative here." He raised his eyebrows.

"I am definitely groping around in the dark!" she confessed with a laugh. He joined her with a relaxed sort of smile and then questioned with a gesture where to put the rocks. She indicated with a nod. "Over there. I'm thinking about bringing the stone wall theme through here with a couple of low terraces. So, I need as many as I can find..."

They worked until dark and when he was leaving, he paused as he opened the door of his ute. "Mum has something for you. She'll drop it over sometime..."

She looked at him. His mother? Why would his mother want to meet her? Mac had nothing to hide, and she could definitely hold her own with any territorial woman. "Oh. I guess I'll be here..."

"I'm going away for a couple of days... so I'll see you when I get back. Finalising some things for Mum."

She looked at him keenly. "Not above running messages for your mother, I see."

"Yeah. But she is my mother... and she asked nicely."

"So, are you saying I didn't ask nicely?"

"Really? Is this still about the food? It's not the same. Family stuff. It concerns me also."

"So..." She shrugged lightly. "So, I'm not a friend, nor a neighbour, nor a local. I must be... the bitchy boss." She laughed lightly, but it sounded harsh, and with it the camaraderie they had shared lugging rocks by the willow all afternoon evaporated.

He said nothing except, "I'll let her know."

And she wondered if he meant the bitchy part. It felt like he did.

৶৹৷৹ৎ

14

She waited for this visitor with the mysterious "something" but when no one came by, Mac quickly forgot about it. She bumped into a number of people in town, and she was getting to know more faces and names. She was walking Frank-L home when Todd skedaddled across her path on a bike and came to a screeching halt. "Hey, how's it going Stampsie?"

"Nearly... Stanzie. It's a hard name. I'm doing well, thank you, Todd."

"Stanzie. We had a running-race at school today. I came second."

"Congratulations! Well done."

"I wanted to win, but I didn't mind too much, 'cause Gull can fly. I tell him that. He's fast."

"Sounds like your friend is quite talented."

"Only in running. I can ride better, and I do tricks on my scooter."

"Wow. That is clever. What's your favourite trick?"

"I can do the one-hander... that's pretty hard. And I'm learning a no-footer. Can your dog do tricks?"

"Well, she's retired now. She used to go to dog-shows."

"I could teach her some tricks. I'm going to get a dog one day." It was a declaration of his qualification to offer such generous help. Stanzie smiled. She wondered why a child had no qualms about teaching an old dog new tricks. Funny how the impossible is possible when you're nine and you don't know the rules.

"I gotta go now. I'm meeting Gull at the servo to cellbrate coming first and second. Gran's going to get us milkshakes," he said as he waved cheerily and peddled off in the dust doing wheelies and skids.

Mac's smile didn't fade all the way home. She enjoyed every time she bumped into Todd at unexpected places. How could one little boy so openly offer her such bighearted goodwill and expect nothing in return? There was that thought... again. Was it always the rule that when she did anyone a favour, it implied she was owed something in return? Did she have the capacity to be a friend just for friends' sake without balancing a ledger?

She let Frank-L off the lead as she walked up the driveway. Iris's little car was parked beside the demountable and she was sitting on the step. Her face lit up as the dog bounded over to her. She stood to her feet and ruffled Frank-L's ears.

"Oh Iris, I hope you have not been waiting long."

"No, not really... my bones were happy for the rest. Been on my feet all day, but it's good to see the shop doing so well. Lots of donations this week."

"Have you got time for a cup of tea?" she said as she opened the door.

"I would love a quick cuppa but I can't stay long."

"You know, I feel almost like I'm settling in. Met a few people today who didn't seem so completely like strangers. It gives me hope,"

"Oh, I think you are quite famous: The lady on the hill... working on the old Guthrie place."

"It sounds quite eccentric. Don't suppose I'll live that down in a hurry."

Iris put on the kettle while Mac quickly stacked away the shopping out of her backpack and cleared a space at the table.

Iris took a small, wrapped package out of her bag and placed it on the table, shrugging in a disarming way. "I mentioned a while ago that I would share with you some personal memories about this cottage," she said, "so this is for you. I hadn't forgotten."

Mac felt like she was six again, sitting at the table beside her birthday cake intrigued by the mystery of the parcel before her. As she ripped the paper, there were four black and white photographs mounted in thin white wooden frames. Mac sat holding the images wordlessly. This was the cottage as it had been: loved and lived in. The first photograph showed sturdy stone-walls; the chimney – tall, straight, and strong; the verandah – shaded and comforting; the trestle in the garden – tended, trimmed and tidy. Standing behind a freshly painted wooden gate, was a couple, smiling in their old age and their dated clothes, presiding over their home-space with great peace.

"They are my Great-grandparents. When they bought this block, it was small compared to how extensive Gumleigh Station was back then. Most people thought they couldn't possibly make a go of it, but Irvin was a strong man and very determined. He came to this district because he'd been told his wife, Adele, would not survive the bleak weather down south. The tragedy is that she didn't. She died a few months before they left. Irvin married my great-grandmother Joanna before they moved. She had been Adele's nurse. They went ahead and relocated for his daughter's sake. He was swindled in the sale; he had thought he had bought a much larger, fertile block. These rocks were all he had to work with. Each one of these stones, he placed himself. The irony is, that if he had had the other place, we would have nothing left to tell this story. This is now five generations of Guthries who have lived in this little house in some way. My grandfather was born in a little donga, while it was being built. He was an avid gardener."

Mac stared at the photo of a man tending a vegetable garden by a willow tree, and the cottage in the background. What a treasure to have original prints like this.

The next photograph was a family portrait with a young teenager standing by a freshly painted scrolled metal gate, in trendy retro flares, platform heels and a bright headband. "That's my Mum and Dad. I was quite the fashion buff," said Iris with a shy smile.

"Iris! You look gorgeous! No wonder Dave fell so hard for you!"

The last one was another family portrait; Iris was standing near the gate again in front of the cottage, with a large bank of flowering irises in full bloom. Her husband beside her and two young boys in tow, one on a bike and the other on roller-skates, both of whom looked impatient to get on with the urgent business of play. Something about that reminded Mac of Todd and she smiled.

Iris took it lovingly and rubbed the ring on her finger. "This is my Dave. He was the best father two boys could hope for." Her voice crackled a little, she swallowed and quickly picked up her bag to leave. Mac thanked her for the gift as she walked her to the door. "When you said you wanted to share something personal, I was a little hesitant... but this is not like that at all. This is just perfect."

"I'm glad you like them. But it is very personal Dear. It is my family. There is nothing more personal in the whole world to me."

"Thank you, Iris. Thank you very much." And she reached out and squeezed her hand.

"Oh. I almost forgot. Dan wanted me to give you this..." Iris passed her an envelope.

"Dan?" She raised her eyebrows and opened it. "Oh... an invitation to dinner." She stared at the address and then looked at Iris. "Why would he invite me to dinner?"

"Perhaps to be friendly?"

She grunted. "Please tell me you will be there."

Iris smiled. "Well, I don't think I have been uninvited. I'm cooking."

When Iris left, Mac stacked the pictures to the side – face down. This home had had a Dad, for generations. She didn't need that just now. But she was excited by what the prints captured of the house and the symbolism of transition and transformation, old to new. What enquiring questions would they generate on her blog about her designs? Immediately she started devising in her mind a visual time-line to hang behind her workspace: these photos leading up to the rundown ruins; the various stages of construction and landscaping; the finished studio: history merging into the present to build the future. She'll find out where Iris bought the frames. The lines were simple and clean.

Mac clenched her jaw as she picked up the invitation. Why wouldn't Dan give it to her in person? It's not like he never sees her. He had refused to be her messenger, but was happy to enlist Iris? Mac wondered if she had ever seen Dan's mother in town. Most likely she had. Anyway, they would meet soon enough. Friday, in fact.

❦⦿⦿❦

Mac sat with her art-pad on her knee studying the photos Iris had given her. She wondered what it would be like to jump into these pictures and be there. What had their garden really been like? They were pieces in an invisible jigsaw that she was part of. She closed her eyes and felt the sun on her forehead; the hum of bees from the hives near the fence; the smell of honeysuckle over the trellis; the vibrant purple of the irises blooming. In her mind she walked around the house feeling the stonewalls, cold under her touch; pinching the herbs from the garden between her fingers; walking under the latticework shaded in fragrant wisteria; hearing the crunch of the gravel under her shoe. She wanted to capture these experiences in a series of paintings, on canvas, to feature in her studio rooms. She could paint them to match her colour palate perfectly.

Then she drew what her garden would become. Not a design, or a cold artist's impression, but a warm, living, sustaining space with Frank-L running along the path. A garden is something that doesn't consume, but restores, refreshes, and grows. It was restoring, refreshing, and growing her.

As always, there was that pragmatic voice niggling away at the dream; constantly needling her to justify them creativity because of the expense. Her work enhanced the street-appeal of this dilapidated little block. It increased its market value! But she knew, deep down, that was not the reason. The reason was the difference it made to her... in her. She had been right to follow her instincts and leave the landscaping until she was occupying the land, rather than getting Carl to map it all out from his office desk. 'Full immersion design' Mockbee admirers would say. She sipped her coffee as she thought about that: occupying. It sounded like an invasion, but it felt much different... like putting something on and wearing it, allowing it to become part of her.

15.

"Oh, I see you have moved some more things in..." said Iris as she pointed to the carton sitting in the corner. "It really does seem you are more settled."

"It's not mine," said Mac clearing her throat. Iris looked at her curiously. "Oh?"

Mac said nothing and brought over a couple of sketches. "What do you think of these? I'm going to put these on canvases for each room. Garden theme... soft edges... reflection. I've based each one around an element of a cottage garden, and ties into my colour board. I'm thinking Kitchen – oregano and sage. Bathroom – Riverstone or in this case Guthrie-stone. And for the other spaces dog-rose, honeysuckle, and irises..."

"Irises?"

"Yes... you have made this place come alive for me. It is my tribute to you. Is that okay?"

"Okay? Oh, my Dear... Dave always had an herb garden by the back door for me and a garden-bed of irises along the path. I feel very humbled."

"Well, I think it is very studio-retreat."

"It sounds 'heritage cottage'... but I thought you were going for unexpected and modern?"

"Unexpected. Yes. But that does not mean I wasn't going to capitalise on the heritage. This is the whole concept of the stone walls... heritage meeting functional-modern.

Besides, you were surprised, so doesn't that make it unexpected?"

Iris lingered over the sketches. "I would say so. Certainly. Your sense of colour... it leaves me feeling... I don't know... sort of rested and satisfied."

"Rested and satisfied?" Mac savoured those words. Why would the opinion of a little lady with no credentials in design be so moving? She smiled sadly and didn't take her eyes of Iris's face. Huh. How about that? It did mean a lot. "The box in the corner is all that is left of my father's things. He died a while ago... probably just after I came here. I wasn't notified until after the funeral."

"Oh, my darling...." Iris stopped and her eyes filled with compassion. She said nothing as she watched Mac go back to her coffee as if she had delivered the trivial news that a shower of rain was expected that afternoon. But there was nothing inconsequential about that box.

Mac shrugged. "I hardly knew him. He left when I was eight."

When Iris left, Mac sat down on the couch and stared at the box. Her lip quivered as she thought about the huge divide between the little girl's dream of Daddy and the jarring reality of it. Why couldn't the illusion go on forever?

ೋ෴ೋ

105

Mac turned into the driveway lined with large camphor laurel trees. The address was a large, elegant brick Federation style bungalow. It had been well maintained and even though there were few apparent renovations to modernise it, she wasn't too ashamed of the overall effect. It had the quality of a solid country home.

She stood on the porch for a moment before she knocked. There was a rather chipped little gnome standing beside the welcome mat like a doorman. That didn't really seem like Dan. Iris answered the door with a glorious smile. "Welcome Dear. We are so delighted to return the hospitality you have given us so many times."

Mac blinked, standing on the front step. "You live here? Oh." She coughed, a little embarrassed. "I thought this was Dan's place."

"It is. Yes. It's his home too."

"Here? He boards with you?"

Iris looked at her with patience and lowered her voice as if sharing a magnificent secret. "Yet, as we both know, he is very independent. I think you would agree he is not attached to my apron strings at all."

"Apron strings?"

"When my Dave passed, I really struggled being in this house all by myself. It was Dan's idea to come back home and use this as a base to work from. I know there is something of a stigma of a grown man choosing that, but family is family. He reminds me of that."

She spluttered and kind of choked. "Family? You are his mother?"

"Ever since I gave birth..." Iris's eyes suggested a bit of mischief twinkling like a morning star. It faded as amazement started to dawn. "Am I correct in thinking you didn't realise this?"

"Oh, my goodness! I had absolutely no idea! What a mess. You are his mother?"

"Yes..." Now Iris looked dazed.

Dan poked his head around the corner. "Are you two going to come in or spend all night 'doing coffee' on the front porch? We do have chairs." He paused and gave a crooked sort of smile. "What's going on? Everything, all right?"

Mac cleared her throat. "Hmm. Iris has just told me she is your mother."

He laughed and looked at her quizzically. "No way! That could explain a whole lot of things!"

Mac scowled. "This is so embarrassing. How could I not know that?"

Every so often, through dinner, Mac stopped chewing and sort of choked, shaking her head, and muttered, "Family?" Then she would groan, and blush, and try to swallow.

After dinner, Iris poured the coffee and offered Mac a chocolate from a gift box that she had on the sideboard. "How are you feeling Dear?"

"Hmm. Not sure," she said sheepishly.

"Well, we would like you to come into the lounge. There is something... Perhaps bring your coffee and lets just sit for a while."

Mac nudged Dan as they went into the next room. "What's this about?" she whispered to him on the side.

"You'll see soon enough. I trust it is nothing as awful as finding out I have parents."

Mac rolled her eyes. Really. This was too much. She'll be the butt of everyone's joke forever. She sat deep in the club lounge and sipped her coffee wordlessly. Just more evidence she didn't fit.

She hardly even looked up when Iris cleared her throat gently. "Dear... we wanted to invite you to dinner, because well, this is more than just friends catching up. I wanted to ask something of you. A sort of... favour." Her voice trailed off. Mac's attention came back to the moment. She looked around the muted light of the room, classic in its setting, but conventional in its taste. Her eyes rested on something covered in a large sheet, sitting in front of the mantle-piece. "Yes – that is it. Would you take a look at it, Dear?"

Mac flinched. It felt uncomfortable. She had been asked to give her opinion on things before, and then people got all offended because she had a tendency to be honest. Compulsion really. She put her coffee down and went over and gently lifted aside the cover. "Oh, my goodness, this is amazing! Who did this?" she exclaimed as she tugged the sheet completely out of the way. There was an outdoor settee made from natural timbers that were polished to a smooth sheen, each branch entwined in its natural shape to form the backrest, arms, legs and the curve of the base.

She looked over at Dan sitting on the lounge, quietly watching her with appreciation. He nodded and said, "You like it then?"

"Absolutely! This is incredible. Did you make this?"

"Guilty as charged," he said.

"This is great. Simple, organic, crafted. You could seriously get good commissions on these pieces. Functional and interesting!"

Dan chuckled and their eyes connected as Mac laughed in her enthusiasm. She didn't have to be ashamed of her honesty here. It was good design and balance; technically well executed.

Iris had a glorious smile on her face. "Do you think you would have a place to put something like this?"

"Oh yes! Definitely! You're offering this to me? How much do you want?"

Dan was quick. "It's not for sale."

"Are you sure? I had some budgeting for custom items. I could look at that."

"Nah. I'm sure. Not for sale. I made it for someone in particular. A gift."

"Oh. Well, that is disappointing. Could I get a quote then... and commission one? This would be perfect under my willow-tree arbour. It would fit so well in that outdoor terraced area... a reflection space."

Iris cleared her throat. "Well Dear, when Dan said it was a gift, it is. We want you to have it: from the original Guthrie family. I hoped it might be like a tribute, acknowledging those who lived there before."

"Me? You just said..." Dan had not moved. She stared at him hard. He sat on the lounge, his face unreadable. "I'm not sure I understand..."

"A gift."

"For me? You made this for me?"

"Yeah."

She traced the lines of the polished branches as they intertwined and meshed in impeccable alignment. Absolutely perfect.

ﷻ

Dan came and sat with her under the tree.

"This is perfect.

"I think the bench works. What is the official verdict now it is in place?"

Mac swallowed. It was incredibly generous. "I... I don't know..."

"Don't know? You don't like it now?"

"No. No! Of course, I like it. It's just... well, it's the idea that you made it particularly for me. That feels awkward..."

110

"Kinda thought we explained that. You're doing Mum a favour... like she said, from the family. The price is a plaque, but I'm sure we can put that somewhere inconspicuous if that is what you prefer." He was hoping against hope she would not refuse the gesture. It meant a lot to his Mum. His Mum. Yes.

He watched her run her hands over the timber in admiration, following the lines of the polished grain as the branches interlaced. He swallowed.

Mac was thoughtful. Something tightened in her chest. So, the bench was just about his mother... Iris. Fair enough. "Dan, why didn't you give me that invitation yourself? I just don't get the whole cloak and dagger thing."

"Goodness, it was from both of us. I thought I told you Mum was going to drop it around. She was dead set on it being a proper invite. She thought that was something that appealed to you, since you invited us to your slab-pouring party."

"Well! If it was so obvious, how could I miss it?"

"Mum told you she was cooking."

"Yes, but Iris cooks for everyone... even strangers building studio apartments. How was I to know she wasn't just helping out a hopelessly, culinary-clueless builder friend?"

"Hey I can cook! I just don't enjoy it that much. Why would I deprive her from all the joy she gets from doing it?" He grinned.

"You could have just told me she is your mother. I met her as the lady from the Op-shop."

He shrugged. "You're having coffee all the time. How could I know you hadn't actually connected us? I'm a bit disappointed to find out you never talked about me though. I assumed I would be a hot-topic... her favourite son..."

"And the male-ego never fails to assert itself."

"We arrived together to that pouring-concrete-breakfast-thing you did."

"We call that car-pooling where I come from!" She closed her eyes and sighed. "I just can't get over it. You even look like family. How could I not see that?"

"Well," he conceded, "I guess you can't know what you aren't told."

Then she gasped. "The food! You were eating Iris's food! You live with your mother, and you still would not mention the food!"

"Are you ever going to give up about the food? That was especially because I live at home. I don't need to get involved when it doesn't concern me."

"But you are involved. You're her son!"

"Doesn't matter if I'm local, royal or kin. It was your food."

"So, the acquisition of privilege is not by being local, or even by being family? The prospect of ever breaking in here seems to get grimmer all the time."

So. She wanted to fit in after all. It surprised him that he was encouraged by that thought. "I guess a lot of stuff is taken for granted when you've grown up in a place. I forget it isn't obvious that we're all related somehow... even by experience."

"Sounds in-bred."

He nodded. "You know you're a Gumleigh local when you have to have your tail surgically removed. Connections make people fiercely loyal. We are never just dealing with neighbourhood geography... we're talking family. That's a pretty strong thing around here."

She smiled weakly. "So, what other secrets am I not privy to?"

"Well, that would mean I could read minds. I'm guessing that's a skill I'm not going to acquire any time soon. Happy to keep clarifying the old-fashioned way though."

She sighed and turned her attention back to the bench. "You are shocking, Dan Henry. And talented. This is very generous. Thank you."

He relaxed and exhaled. "I was started to think you might have had second thoughts about keeping it."

"I'd have to be nuts to turn this away. It's gorgeous."

"Every piece turns out differently, but I particularly liked the way this one came together. Still, I wasn't too sure how it would go for you. It's a bit raw for some tastes... those who like straight lines and edges."

"And you think I am a straight line and edge person?"

"Well, it is pretty well established that you are sort of particular."

"Really? 'Particular'?" She laughed at him.

"Ah-huh... but when I found you down here under the willow working on your arbour. In the dirt... not looking straight and tidy... I thought it might not be too weird. This is something that hasn't a straight line to its name. Mum's been onto me about it. She can be a veritable nag," he said affectionately.

"Well, the bit about it not getting weird didn't work... because this is totally weird. Iris is your mother! I'm sure I've said stuff... about how impossible you are."

He smiled. "Guess it was inevitable that my plot to infiltrate the life and mind of Constance McIntosh would eventually be exposed. Such a waste: all that effort."

"Cute. I can see Iris has espionage qualities." She grinned and covered her eyes. "I thought she was like seventy years old. How awkward is that?"

He grinned. "Really? That is the stuff of blackmail. I could use that..."

She smiled charmingly "Blackmail – to what end? I don't have millions."

He considered her for a moment. Did he dare? "There is one thing that would be worth it," he said tentatively.

"Yeah right. I have a good lawyer, and I am not afraid of a barney, so be warned how you pick your fights Dan Henry."

"Okay," he said straightening up. "You're on. I am going to fight you on this one." He waited for her to look at him. When she did, she saw sober earnestness in his eyes.

"You're sick! You gift me the most amazing bench-seat and the next thing you are trying to pick a fight... and you would put my friendship with Iris into the mix!"

He said nothing as he looked at her flashing eyes. How could she so easily twist what he meant? She didn't even ask what was so important to him. Oh boy. But Dan was tenacious enough to stick out a fight. He could tackle anything she could possibly bring on. Still, he hesitated. He wasn't sure what he was fighting for... the principle or just to see how much was in her. He was definitely curious about that too.

She stood up and stared at him. "Well, I'm happy to oblige. Try your hardest, Dan Henry. I am up for it."

His gaze went from her eyes to the grim line of her lips. "I think I actually believe you. You're going to fight me on this the whole way. You'd do well to prepare for the battle of your life. You may be surprised what this is about." He stood up and walked back to where his vehicle was parked. He rubbed his chin thoughtfully. He hadn't expected that... that was for sure. Did he really want to go there? The woman was as unstable as the San Andreas Fault line. Tragic but true.

~ ❦ ~

Iris came and sat with Mac on the bench. They sat silently for a time, watching the sway of the breeze in the long green leaves. "I wondered if it would be alright if I came here sometimes... just to sit?"

Mac raised her brows. She was surprised she was not the only one affected by the compelling lure of this place. For all its ugliness, it seemed to hold a magnetic pull. "Sure. I forget that this tree is familiar to you. Could you see it from your windows?"

"The kitchen. I used to come here a bit... at a particular time. Seemed appropriate then." This tree certainly had a long history as a thinking place.

"Oh..."

"It took a long time for us to fall pregnant. Then when we did... twice I was... and we lost them early on. Too early to tell. I was so angry... and then so sad. It was here that I would come and tell them that I loved them, that I was sad that I didn't get to see them growing up. I gave up thinking I would ever be a mother... and then my miracles came along... straight after each other. Just like that. I always felt this old tree celebrated my miracles, because she had grieved with me for so many years. Dan used to climb these branches. It was a happy place too."

Stanzie shuddered, and quietly stared at the twisted trunk. "How could you give this up? There are so many personal memories here."

"I haven't given anything up... my memories are not held by the geography, but the places in my heart. I've long got used to that idea. When I was young, I couldn't get out of Gumleigh fast enough. But when we came back it was home... because Dave was with me. Then I had to let go again when we realised that maintaining the house was too much. Just watching it in ruins was harder perhaps. That's why we put it on the market."

"Why didn't you say something right at the start? I didn't realise. What if I had decided to bulldoze the whole site, or rip the tree out? It would all be gone forever."

"I cannot tell you how excited I was to see that you are preserving these special aspects of this place. Here you have a little refuge where people can come and rest and think and heal. This is so appropriate. It is like another miracle."

"Did you ever name them? Your babies?"

Iris's eyes filled. "I did... sort of... in my mind. I never told anyone, but I chose unisex names because I didn't know. The first was Alex, and then Toni. I still remember those dates. That's a connection I'll always have. I like to think there was a boy and a girl, but I don't know. I've often wondered what it would be like to be a mother of a girl... growing up to be a woman. I hope that she would be like you."

The silence wrapped around them, in a cloak of comfort.

⸙

16.

Mac was dressed in jeans and work-boots, holding, and fetching. She found building tedious and slow. The actual construction... it didn't feel at all creative, like she expected. She was used to checking in on a job every day and seeing the vision materialise. She was used to keeping it on track. She was used to ensuring tradesmen had not opted for sloppy short-cuts and she was used to telling them how to do their job properly. This was different. Measuring tapes and nails had as much appeal to her as driving on holidays and whinging to her mum, "Are we there yet?" It reminded her of standing under the washing line as a kid watching her soft rabbit drying, pegged up by his ears. That day lasted forever. Or it was like baking. Decorating the cake was more her style than mixing it up and peering through the glass oven door until it was cooked. The metaphors kept coming. And what's more, Dan's systematic fastidious attention to detail outshone her pedantic surveillance of any project.

Was it because she was essentially a big-picture person? Yet her artwork held such detail. An inkling goaded her mind that the intolerance she had borne towards budget conscious clients had been uncompromisingly harsh. When financial constraints sacrificed art for practical it was always a personal insult. She had become that client. She had to let some things slide for the greater scope of the project.

She was talking over some of the adjustments that impacted her budget items as they worked. Not really making conversation; more just thinking out loud. Dan acknowledged her calculations every so often with a grunt and indicated with a nod where he needed a beam held. He positioned the nail gun. "Is everything about money?"

Mac hated it when he did that. She felt attacked and prickly when he questioned her motives. She fired up, perhaps because it was just more interesting to be fired up.

"There would be no dilemma if it was just about money, or if it was just about design and art. But it's not. The two coexist. The tension is always present."

He grinned amiably. "I like it when we talk."

That was annoying. "That's absurd. I've been talking to you all morning. You're the only one here!"

He met her gaze and smirked. "Yet now I feel included in the conversation."

"How was I not including you? You're building my house! We're not going to get much done if we spend the time staring each other down."

He fired off two nails and moved around a bearer. "So, you're saying nothing can happen without the mighty buck? What if the Bible is right, and one cannot serve both God and Mammon? In a world where this tension between the bottom-line and the artistic coexists, is that even possible?"

"Mammon?"

"Bible for 'Moolah'."

"Humph. Tell me. Why do you build? Is it money or the satisfaction generated by the process of creating something? I'll bet my bottom dollar you wouldn't be here if I didn't pay."

He raised his eyebrows. "I am in the providential position of doing something I find satisfying... which also happens to allow me to eat. It's not either/or... but 'and'. This and that."

"I rest my case. They coexist. But ultimately you do what you do because it pays. Money. You're merely a mercenary for hire. And unfortunately, it always dictates the extent of art. It's so frustrating that this is the case. I have condemned people for compromising on their dream. Yet holding true to purist architectural forms rarely is possible because of finances. But I'm beginning to think the motivation is not a moral question... but just the climate in which the moral exists. It is a climate we are all subject to. I don't know any one for who it doesn't apply."

"Of course, you do." Two more nails.

"Nup. Not even one."

"Volunteers." Two more nails. "Like my mother." Two more nails. He enjoyed playing the devil's advocate. "She does what she does because she wants to. Not because she is financially motivated. She doesn't have to, yet she chooses to. They say the country runs on volunteers like her: people who do stuff to give something back." Two more nails.

"You miss the point. She doesn't 'have to' because the money question is already sorted for her. If it wasn't, she would be dictated by money... yet again."

Mac held on to the beam she was holding, her knuckles turning a shade lighter. Dan grabbed another plank, measured, and sawed. She said nothing while he positioned the timber, adjusted, and nailed. He stood back then and stretched his arms, rolling his shoulders. She put down the wood she was holding. "I need a break," she said abruptly and walked off, muttering as she opened the toilet cubical door.

When she came back, he glanced up from what he was doing. "Grab that for me, will you?" She sat down on a sawhorse. He was about to repeat it, when he stopped. "What's up?"

"You are so provoking."

"Hmm? That sounds personal." Well, evidently some topics were off limits. Something to note.

She took a breath. Just say it. "I don't think this is... working. You said we would re-evaluate periodically: Well, I think you should get your labour-hire. That way I can focus on the landscaping. Working on both areas together will probably save money in the long run." She flinched. Every rationale she gave, really was about money. But she didn't have the liberty of that volunteer option. It had to be factored.

Dan put down his tools and sat on his haunches. "This is kinda sudden."

"No, not really. I've been thinking about it since you were finishing off at the Motel. I had time to work on the landscaping then and it was good for me, working out there. That is what I want to concentrate on. And even if it does cost more... I want to do that."

"Oh." He watched her for a while. "You have guts you know."

She blinked. "I thought you would say I was avoiding you."

"Are you?"

"No, of course not. I'll be here. You can ask me anything you need. I can run some of the off-site errands. It might work smoother having an extra pair of hands." Avoidance was the pay-off. That was also true.

"Fair enough. You call the shots. Done. You'll still have to work a couple of days until I can be sure I've got someone."

"That's it?"

"I can't think of anything else. Did you think there might be more?"

"You didn't object. Don't you like working with me?"

"I didn't sack you; I haven't pulled a red-card on you once. Why would you think I don't like working with you?"

"Because you seemed relieved."

"Well, I'm not. This is your call. Your decision, not mine. No point haggling over something when your mind is set. I know that about you at least."

"Oh." Ned had said that. She felt that she had run herself up a blind alley and didn't like the view. "Why did you say I had guts?" she asked quietly.

He paused and considered her. Yep. This time he could be honest. "I'm guessing this is a decision that is not just bottom-line. You are willing to cop the extra wages, but more than that, you're going out on a limb to trust me with this. This job is extremely personal for you. It says to me that you trust me to get on and do what needs to be done here, so you can do what you need to do out there. I don't think that is an easy thing. Takes courage."

"You think I off-sided because I don't trust you?"

"Proximity offers more control perhaps."

"I'll still be watching."

"I hope so."

"Really?"

Oh boy. What was he doing? "Yep. Really. Grab that for me, will you?" and he went back to work.

17.

While Dan and his offsider continued on the studio, Mac became totally immersed in the landscaping. Sometimes she had some labourers come in and help but mostly it was easier to do it herself... at her own pace. Mac hadn't done much landscaping design in the past. Tommy insisted Carl exclusively did the landscaping work. "That's why I employ him," he would say. Still, Carl encouraged her, and they often were spitballing landscaping concepts on big projects. It was only natural for her to show him her studio retreat and he replied with a couple of solid recommendations to bring cohesiveness to the whole block. Carl certainly knew plants. So, she ordered his recommendations to be ready for collection according to her timeline. She had deliveries of gravel, sand, rocks, and mulch coming as well.

Mac threw herself into the digging and the shaping and the moving. She stockpiled the rocks as they were unearthed. The front was almost complete. She was surprised it wasn't the building that was freeing up her stiff emotions like physio, but the garden. Never before had she needed to set reminders to go to a work-site to check it was going according to plan. She would walk around, pick up a few off-cuts and decide if they were reusable or throw them in the rubbish skip, and wander off. On one inspection, Dan downned tools and came over. "Just checking... is everything okay?" he said.

Mac looked around and shrugged. It seemed fine. She felt removed, unmoved. This type of work had been her passion forever; this particular dream had been held sacredly for a long time. And now it was here, under construction, and for the life of her she couldn't understand why working in the garden had more appeal, more pleasure, more anticipation, more enchantment than this. It didn't make sense. Was she losing her drive? Was she losing her sense of priorities? Was she losing herself? If this wasn't her, she almost didn't know who she was.

"With the building? Seems on track..."

"And with you?" He looked at her mildly.

The question was kind of unnerving. "Fine. Why wouldn't it be fine?"

"Just checking," he said. "So, I have a few questions. Are you up for a coffee after you finish this afternoon?"

"Oh. Umm..." Had she lost her ability to make a decision? "Sure. If you need to..."

"Would be helpful I think." Helpful? Who in their right mind says coffee is 'helpful'? He swallowed. He was talking about clarifying his questions. Of course.

"Okay then." She looked away. That felt weird. She returned to finishing marking out some areas before the bobcat contractor came to do the major contouring for the

back yard. Oh. She had forgotten to mention that. Oh well.
Dan could wait if things were delayed.

Just on morning-tea time, a truck rolled up with the
bob-cat. Mac was in the donga making a cup of coffee, which
she usually took back with her to where she was working. She
looked out the window as the operator jumped from the cab.
The way he did that seemed familiar. "Morning Mac," Ned
said cheerily as she came over.

"Oh. You." She stared at Ned in dismay. This man was
responsible for her contouring?   He was walking around
locking ramps in place.

"You're on time," she accused

"No traffic accidents this morning," His eyes laughed
at her acknowledging his story was open slather for ridicule.
It obviously didn't bother him any. It was beyond her that the
man held no shame.

She was about to offer that thought out loud when she
heard another voice behind the truck call, "Frank-L!" Todd
ran out laughing as Frank-L bounded up to him, and licked
his hand, sniffing the ball he held. Todd threw it, and Frank-
L dashed away to retrieve. She looked from Todd whom she
adored, to Ned whom she despised, and realised Todd's
freckles and the gingery tones to his hair was probably
genetic. "Father and son, I presume."

She watched Frank-L trailing after Todd. He stopped
then and yelled out, "Hey Uncle Dan!" and ran over to the
worksite.

"Yo! Up here!" He called from a ladder. "Wait there. Coming down." He climbed down and scooped him up. Laughing.

"Uncle?" She glared at Ned. "You're his brother?" His eyes were laughing at her again. "Nope. You were right the first time. He's my son. He's nine."

She sighed. It was a realisation. "Dan Henry is your brother. Oh really?"

"Honestly. What was he thinking?" Ned said in scandalised tones.

"The bob-cat is not yours." She looked at the truck where it was loaded.

He looked at her keenly and then shrugged. "Actually, it is. But does it matter? It'll still do the work."

"That bob-cat is the same one Dan used to clear the site. He told me he shared it... with a partner." She was not deterred. She was putting it together. "Brother, partner, boss. Dan is the one you referred to as your boss. He's the obnoxious boss!"

"Anyone who knows Dan would hardly say he is obnoxious."

"But your partner is Dan?"

"Guessing that is not a question."

"Oh, I have a lot of questions!"

"No doubt." Seriously. Where was she going with this? "Look. Is this going to affect what you want done? Because I can go..."

"Oh no you don't! I've booked you. And I'll pay you in case there is any doubt."

"No problem then. Just show me your plans."

"But there was no obnoxious boss at all, was there?" she insisted.

"Like I said, I would never accuse Dan of that." He shrugged. This woman was way too stuffy. He found everything about her quite ridiculous, and an endless source of amusement.

She shook her head. Then another connection was made. "Iris! Iris is your mother? But she's so lovely."

There was really no response to be made to that either. "What can I say? It runs in the family. I'll unload," he said and left.

Mac walked over to where Dan and Todd were looking at his power-tools. Todd stood up and grinned. "Hey Stanzie," he said. "Uncle Dan says this is a pretty neat house you're building."

"I'm glad he thinks so."

"Stanzie?" Dan raised his eyebrows and looked bemused. "So, Stanzie, you've met my nephew, Todd?"

"Apparently. I just knew him as Todd, the-owner-of-a-very-cool-scooter. Just like I know Ned, as the part owner of a bobcat, truck-driver, neander..." She glanced at Todd. "...operator, general carrier... who is, as it turns out, also your brother. Is there any one in town you're not related to?

He thought about that for a second. "Well, Stanzie, I think we talked about this. I've had my tail surgery. But now that you mention it, I don't think there is any family connection with Old Mrs Riley over on Drover Street."

"Very funny."

"Very true... Stanzie."

She frowned and rolled her eyes. He was really very immature sometimes. "I think it is time to contact Ned's obnoxious boss so I can have those carefully selected words with him," she said pointedly.

"Hey Todd – want to grab my esky out of the Ute? Smoko-time. Some of Gran's biscuits in there for you... there are coconut jam-drops." Todd took off and Dan turned back. "What's this about?"

"You said you wanted to be in on that conversation. Now's your chance."

"So, you've met my brother. He off-sides sometimes when the other jobs are slow, and I need an extra hand. I'm not his boss actually... partners."

"Actually, I figured that out. Did you really tell Ned to load the cubical back on the truck! How could you?"

Dan looked at her carefully. It felt like Ned had just framed him for murder by dusting his fingerprints all over the weapon. "I'm sorry if you feel that the way we do business is not ethical. It wasn't personal." It was inevitable that he would be convicted, sentenced, condemned, and executed.

"Well, let me just say it jolly-well felt personal when he was driving away with my ensuite!"

"And I have it on good authority as an employer, I'm not terrible. Bob tells me I am a fair boss."

"Really? And what would Bob know?'

"In the interests of a full disclosure, the Hardware is our family business. Partners... with Ned the Neanderthal."

"Bob doesn't own it?"

"Manager." He pointed to his chest, and then across to where Ned was working. "Boss."

"Grief! You've got a finger in every Gumleigh pie! Why didn't you let me know you are Ned's brother?"

"Because it's irrelevant. Ned could be my Great Uncle Thadeus; it makes no difference. He turned up. Did your job. We got paid. Contract closed." He looked at her and shook his head. "I can't believe you introduced yourself to Todd as Stanzie." It was more an accusation than an observation.

"Well, believe it. You want irrelevant. You've got it. It makes no difference what Todd knows me by!"

Dan watched as Todd started back with his esky, munching on a biscuit. "This is not done..." he said through a gritted smile as he turned towards Todd.

She shrugged. "Well, I'm done. I have a contractor waiting to start work." She stalked off, and explained the plans in very clipped, short sentences, where the terracing was to be done; the filling and cut-out work along the contour of the path and gardens; and the pond near the willow. Ned gave her a cheery thumbs-up and went to work.

She sighed and sat down on the willow-bench. This was wrong. Wrong. All wrong! She felt like Alice, where nothing was as it seemed. She pictured Dan sitting opposite her at the servo, grinning at her over coffee while she vented about Ned's little stunt. Then there was the generator fiasco. She felt humiliated and all he was doing was carrying on about her name! What was getting into him? She could decide who was privy to which version of herself. That was her prerogative. Somehow Todd had skipped a dozen of those versions, straight to her heart.

Perhaps that was it. Dan was polite, guarded. Unnaturally so. It was weird that this was the first time she had actually seen him annoyed. It was strange that it had nothing to do with business or the building project, but her name.

Ned had obviously used the boss charade as theatrics for the female city-slicker. He probably didn't even call Dan on the phone. Yet, Dan didn't deny any of it. And the funny thing was, because he wasn't defensive, it reinforced her suspicions he hadn't been part of it. She had no issue with Dan's ethics, since he brought that up. It was more that things seemed shrouded. Who ever knew what Dan Henry was thinking... or feeling... or wanting? Certainly not her! She just wanted to be mad at him. Damn Dan Henry. He was infuriating!

She internally braced herself. She needed to make the most of the time the bobcat was at her disposal. Mac took a deep breath. The dust of the gravelly ridge contrasted to the smell of rich loam being turned down by the creek. Somehow that helped her to feel more grounded. Back to work.

Something else had been bothering her. The stonemason was booked, but she was pretty sure she would run out of stone. Even though the house stood on this rocky outcrop, it seemed that generations of Guthries had pretty much used most of the usable surface rock from the immediate area around the block. The stone pillars in the front driveway would use most of the stone from the wall and chimney they had deconstructed. It seemed ironic that if she was going to continue the rock-wall theme through the garden, down to the willow tree, then she'd have to import more rock. And that was more cost.

The afternoon flew quickly. For all of Ned's blasé cheeriness, Mac reluctantly acknowledged he was a competent operator, manoeuvring the mini excavator into awkward corners so that in a short time she could see the form of the garden taking shape. They moved the bench seat, and she stood back as a small area was levelled for her arbour; a ditch was hollowed out for her pond. Another area flattened for her chook run. She allocated a larger pad for her potting shed, a working space, not just for storing gardening tools. In keeping with the theme, she had wanted the potting shed to have one stonewall, with timbered walls like the main house. Perhaps she could save those rocks and trellis some ivy instead across the windowless wall. That might work.

Her timeline was on track. She moved her bench out of the way and sat down reviewing her items, ticking off different to-do's on her tablet; adjusting and expanding the list as she went.

"Ahem." Dan cleared his throat as he sat down and handed her a coffee from Snook's café bar. "Coffee as planned."

"Oh. That time already?" She really didn't want to do this now. She was in project-mode; this was foremost in her mind. It had to be. "Ned's nearly done. I'll just see where he's up to." She put down the coffee and nearly bolted to where he was heading back to reload the truck.

Dan watched her go. He knew what she thought of his brother. No magnetism there. What about him? Were they two south poles who would never connect? He looked curiously at the tree and drank his coffee while he waited. The willow was a familiar part of this place. Mac was right: it didn't seem to fit her concept of the studio. Yet now it was starting to. Now it was part of the working design, and there was no going back. There was something intensely interesting about the way she had twisted her way into his heart. It. The tree. He was grateful she was not going to bulldoze it. But if Stanzie got it in her head that that's what she was going to do, what hope did he have?

Stanzie. He thought that contraction of Constance really suited her. Constance even more. 'Mac': that was hard... tough... even butch... so un-Stanzie. And the more he got to know her, she wasn't those things. It annoyed him no end that she would introduce herself as Stanzie to a nine-year-old, even if he was a kid he loved. All he was given after months of working with her was 'Mac'.

He sighed and picked up her coffee. He went back to the work site and found her sitting on a saw-horse in the studio. Ned had gone. "Your coffee's getting cold..."

She took it. She felt tired. She didn't want to fight through the mist and the fog of politeness anymore. She didn't want to justify herself again and again. Take it or leave it. How could she explain that? She took a sip, her eyebrows arching in a fine curve. "Caramel? Oh, that is good. Thanks."

"Snooks remembered you liked that. Ordered it in."

"She did? Huh. She doesn't look like a 'details' person."

"Lots of people are not what they seem. First impressions are not always accurate perhaps."

She looked up at him and felt like crying. This was nuts. Never. Not in front of him. He wanted polite. Well, she could do that too. "Hmm. My first impression of Ned was pretty spot on." Actually, she knew she had been a tad harsh. His work was really good.

"I've known him longer, I guess. Just saying, some impressions can change. You, for example... you introduce yourself as Mac. It seems there is more to you than that. Yet you insist on it."

The name thing. Again. It was like he believed a name could be right or wrong. "Mac is something my clients and colleagues call me. It is simple and short and easy to remember."

"I do have the capacity to remember somebody's name," he chipped.

"I have no idea what you are annoyed about."

"Just because I wield a hammer for a living doesn't mean I'm a plank short of a full load. You treat me like the village idiot."

"Oh, come on! Stanzie is reserved for family, friends. Of which you have made it eminently clear you are not. I would hate to confuse that understanding by presuming you might call me something that was too familiar." Right back at you Dan Henry, she thought grimly.

"Familiar? To call you by name? As someone once said to me – we're not sleeping together. It's your name."

"Only certain people get to be that familiar."

"You don't trust me?"

"You're building my studio. I know very few I would trust so implicitly."

"Just the building? What about us?"

"Us? What about us? Tell me Dan, what is there beyond the dotted line? It seems to me that I know nothing about your life. I didn't have a clue who your mother was...

or apparently your brother... or your business manager. Whenever I've wanted to explore beyond that line I've been reigned in very quickly. Now that I've kept to it, it seems I'm being convicted of a felony. It can't be both ways."

"Okay then. Ask me any question."

"Give me a break. You have no idea. You're cracked if you think an inquisition is going to open up real conversation. You can't strap me onto a medieval stretching rack, poking hot irons through my eyes and expect connection!"

"Huh! You feel like you're being tortured! Apparently, that goes both ways." He sat down opposite her, perched on another sawhorse. He was really uncomfortable, stretched way beyond what he was used to. But he had already decided this was the something he would fight for. That fight was expanding. Damn. He took a breath and another... and then retreated to work. Safe. "I do genuinely have some questions about the job. Can we talk about those? Please."

She nodded, relieved that the emotion ebbed away, and she could retreat into that common ground. They could work together. That was obvious. Whether they could relate beyond that was less apparent and untested. She had no idea... whether she could, or even wanted to.

❧ ❧

18.

The concrete was poured for the arbour and when the seat was finally positioned on the pad, they sat in the shade of the tree having a late lunch. Mac looked over at Dan. "Remember how you said I could ask you any question? Well, I have one."

He raised his eyebrows. "Okay."

"My question is this: Now you are working within my design, what do you really think of it? Honestly."

Damn. She was never going to choose personal. It was always about the job. He didn't look up but continued to eat his burger. "I've already answered that. The day we met I told you what I thought. That's a first impression that hasn't changed."

"But you said it was interesting!"

Huh. She had remembered that. "Yes," he said. "I did."

Mac was disgusted. "Interesting is like saying Mozart is elevator music. Or Turner is pop-art... or Utzon suburban... the four-minute mile a stroll. It doesn't allow for the exceptional... or talent, or passion even. No one has ever called my work interesting!"

He smiled and shook his head as if amazed and took a bite of his burger.

"You think I am pinning tickets on myself to say that?" she said. "I have won awards. One doesn't get that sort of recognition for just for being mildly interesting."

His grin became broader as he cracked open his can of coke with a shake of his head.

"What's so amusing?"

"I am just curious that that is what you heard."

"I heard it because that is what you said!"

Then he looked at her. "No. That is what you heard." She snorted in disgust and turned away. Without shifting his gaze, he waited until she looked back at him.

"What?"

"Would you like to know what I said?" he offered. She inhaled as her eyes locked into his. "Okay..." she said.

Without moving he said, "Interesting is piquing my curiosity; stimulating my wonder; being amazed about what could be next. It is like looking through a telescope... or a microscope... being introduced to new realms that I never knew existed. Interesting is an invitation to absorb a panoramic vista... or to notice the intriguing patterns on the underbelly of a mushroom; seeing the symmetry of design and the genius of creativity passionately joined... like marriage. Interesting."

She laughed. "You think my work is like sex?"

"Marriage. There is a difference."

"Oh wow. Wow!"

"Interesting..."

"I think I just fell in love." "With what?"

"With you."

He smiled and absorbed that idea for a moment. "I'm sure you will get over that. I doubt you think me that interesting." And he gathered up his tool belt and went back to the site. Mac looked mystified at his leftover burger, his half-finished can of coke and realised she was holding her breath, and she slowly relaxed her diaphragm.

∾⁊

19

Iris stood by Mac's kitchen counter and sipped her tea. "I'm so glad you have decided to come. I think you will quite enjoy our little Christmas church service."

"I thought you would go to the Salvation Army place... since you work for them at the Op Shop."

"I like to think of Christian churches as all part of the same village... just living in different houses. I chose my church based on where I am most comfortable worshiping. Our church feels like home."

"Comfortable? I thought religious people had to do hard, unpleasant things."

Iris smiled. "You have the most interesting perspectives dear."

Mac snorted. There was that word again.

Iris continued. "I don't think I choose hard, unpleasant things on purpose, but when it is like that, I feel God closest to me... and we get through. Together."

Huh. Mum said that. Weird really. When her Mum said things like that it had irritated her. Now she was sort of comforted by it. "My mother found a lot of consolation in religion at the end. But to be honest, I've never thought much about God before. I'm kinda surprised you haven't said too much about it. So, is Dan religious too?" Mac asked.

Stanzie gathered her things as Iris put down her cup. "Depends on what you mean by religious I suppose. But I'm sure you could ask him about it."

"You must know."

"Well, we've adopted a family rule, and we try to stick to it."

"There's a rule about this?"

Iris smiled apologetically. "Well, more a principle perhaps. I don't tell too many people. It can kind of give the wrong impression."

"I promise to be good."

"Essentially, it is that we don't speak for the other person."

"Huh. Explains Dan's aversion to being a messenger-boy."

"When my Dave passed on. I..." Iris's eyes misted up and her lips went firm, and she restlessly rubbed the ring on her finger. "I was not coping at all. I tried to give up... a number of times. It was awful."

Mac stared at her. What Iris was disclosing seemed like she referred to another frail and vulnerable person altogether. Except she was talking in the first-person. Mac only saw her as a strong, resilient, gentle, kind soul... ageless almost, with all her wrinkles. Yet what she was saying was very human with a great many vulnerabilities.

"I lost contact with myself. I would get Dan to make my decisions, do my shopping, arrange my meals, manage my affairs, answer my questions. I did nothing for myself. We went to get some advice, but I didn't appreciate it at all. I became very angry. It was suggested that, although it was okay in a time of crisis, I ultimately had to be able to do things for myself. This person said I was strong enough to take responsibility for my stuff, and I was manipulating Dan by all my neediness. It was more than just getting lazy; it was the way I felt valued with Dave gone. I wanted Dan to take his place. In my desperation to hang onto them both I was pushing Dan away. He was living here but becoming more and more remote. I realised I had a choice, but it was such a huge thing that I didn't know where to start. I felt I could begin with what I said. I had to get to know who I was all over again... and allow Dan to be Dan. He had to stop protecting me. I had to do my own stuff. Until I got started, I had no idea how many things I was relinquishing. It was hard to keep to it, but with some help, it has become pretty standard now."

Mac stared at her friend. Who knew that she didn't just arrive at being this gentle, together sort of person, but had worked so hard?

"Oh, I'm sorry Dear... Christmas. It's one of those hard, unpleasant times for me. It's the day I miss my Dave the most. It's meant to be a happy time. By this evening I will be back on track. I'm looking forward to tonight."

"It's a relief, to hear you say that. I've been dreading this day too."

"Oh yes, Dear... your Mum."

She nodded and deflected before she teared up. "Is this why you cook so much?" Iris had her ways of coping; she wondered what hers were.

"It's part of it, I guess. It was a way I found to look outside myself. But I know I can over do it because I have this tendency to smother people." She smiled at Mac affectionately. "You have been very patient with me, Dear. Thank you for coming to dinner. We'd never get through it just with our lot."

Mac shook her head amazed. She didn't eat that much. Or was it not just the meal she was referring to? And how extraordinary that Iris was thanking her. She had only thought Iris had helped her... more than cooking meals... more than Christmas dinner... more than Iris would ever understand. "I think we're allowed to miss the people we love. I reckon Mum would like what I'm doing here. I would have loved to show her."

"She would be so proud... and not just with your project."

؈❧☙ℭ☙❧

They arrived at the little church. It was a weatherboard chapel with hard wooden pews; the lines softened only by a wreath of fake holly bordering the communion table and pulpit. It seemed like it was time-locked in the 1930's. It amused Stanzie no end that Iris had been so definite about being comfortable here. They sang traditional carols, read the Christmas story from a big black bible, and took up an offering with wide open-mouthed plates to give to a Christmas charity.

It was just like the little Church she had visited when they went to stay with Aunt Lorna after her birthday. That birthday. Mum said she needed Aunt Lorna. They stayed with her for about six months. She remembered one Sunday there had been a baby christening. The baby was screaming and screaming and screaming at the baptismal font near the front altar. Stanzie had felt so sorry and sad and had cried for that little baby. She had felt so sorry and sad for herself... and wondered why no one cried for her.

Stanzie spent most of the service recalling the details of that other little country church: the dog roses Aunt Lorna had placed on the table by the door; the spider frantically spinning its web in the window frame; the boy in front of her pulling faces at her; her coin rolling out of her hand and falling through a crack in the floorboards. She thought it was a weird introduction to religion. She wondered if that was why God had never seemed to be a serious matter to her. Or too serious. Her mother had certainly taken to reading her Bible again when she was sick. She even said that she had been wrong to neglect God all these years, and sometimes at night, when the pain would not settle, she would find her Mum with her headphones on, quietly singing hymns with tears in her eyes. What about God neglecting her? She had been so devout. She was faithful to God, why wouldn't he do anything for her in the end? The pain had been very bad. It was so unfair! Mum had been a good person. She had been the best.

❧⸙❧

Mac arrived at dinner with a bottle of wine and a bundle of presents. She had been given strict instructions: every gift had to have a card with a short phrase behind its meaning, and she was not allowed to bring food. She was wondering how she would go with Ned in the same room for any length of time. She'd never met Ned's wife and she felt quite self-conscious to be included in this family event. She was introduced to Sandy, and realised she had seen her around town, a teacher at the primary school. Todd quickly monopolised Stanzie's attention with descriptions of wonderful Christmas loot.

She handed around her gifts: a cap with a rather patronising slogan on it for Ned with the exact same thing written on the card. Sandy's card said something quite neutral about the beauty of colour for her hand-painted scarf. Todd's gift was a new helmet and kneepads, and the card with it said, "Bravery is the best protection for every new challenge". Her framed painting of the willow tree for Iris, read on the back: "Memories are the landscape of the soul".

And Dan... when it came to Dan, she had felt lost. In the end she had settled on a telescope, and the little card simply read: "To explore vistas yet unseen..." Todd gave her a chew toy for Frank-L and a limerick about Frankl's ankle. Ned and Sandy's gift of a dog-bed had a comment about best friends and bedfellows. Ned insisted he had wanted to write wisdom such as, "Let sleeping bitches lie," but Sandy wouldn't allow it. Iris gave her a book of inspiring architects, with the Bible verse, Luke 6:48 on the inside: "A builder constructed a house and laid a solid foundation. When the storms came, it could not be shaken for it was built upon The Rock."

Dan's present was in a box. When she lifted it out, it was a table lamp, the base formed from twisted timbers like the willow-tree... and his card read, "Even out of twisted, sad places, light can shine."

Ned rolled with laughter and said that "twisted and sad" trumped the 'bitches' remark he had laboured over all Christmas Eve. Mac smiled and rolled her eyes and offered a benign rejoinder. Today she refused to be annoyed.

And then they tackled the food and tried to put a dint in the Christmas fare Iris had been preparing for weeks.

20.

Stanzie heard a familiar voice start to pray and jolted back to the present. Dan was standing at the front of the church, preparing to preach. She stared at him, gob-smacked. Dan Henry was a preacher? She glanced over to Iris sitting beside her and she didn't look the slightest bit surprised to see him there. Guess that answered the religious question. Stanzie suspected that a builder would not be a very articulate speaker, but then she remembered his definition of "interesting". Then she remembered her comment about sex. Then she remembered her declaration of falling in love. She had only done that once before, and the recipient of that pronouncement could not have been any quicker to seal it with a tender kiss and firm, lively sex. Oh, my goodness! She groaned and sunk low in her pew. How unbelievably humiliating! What on earth did he think of her? He had told her what he thought of her work, but suddenly, what he thought of her as a person was far more significant. No wonder he was unmoved by her declaration, however insincere.

She tried to focus on what he was saying. She raised an eyebrow as he lifted up his handsaw and wood-plane like trusted friends. She looked at his hands, work roughened from handling timber and tools. What was he saying? Jesus was a carpenter? Oh, that was uncanny. She remembered pictures in the books on Aunt Lorna's shelf of Jesus with sheep, so she had supposed he was a farmer. But there had been pictures of fishing boats too. She had been fascinated by all those paintings. How strange. Who would have thought that the Son of God was blue-collar? And then she pictured the art-piece that was sitting down near her willow-tree. That bench had come from timber that had been rough and untamed; but now – from those tools, functional and interesting. More hope glowed.

After the service, Mac filed to the back of the hall for a cup of tea. There was a cake and a batch of Iris's biscuits and a smile from the others. A couple of people asked how the 'reno' was going; and Mac nodded politely and said she had good help. One fellow slapped her on the shoulder so hard she choked on a crumb. "Good is only the best – hey? Our Dan is the best," he laughed good-naturedly. Inwardly she groaned. Her project was hardly a 'renovation', and Dan was getting the credit for being the soul of its success. Was there really any point building an exclusive studio in a place like Gumleigh? How could she possibly get the publicity and mileage it deserved? She deserved. And then she turned away and looked at the coloured vintage glass in the windows and reprimanded herself. This was not why she was here. She could have stayed close to civilization if her goal was to build something that would become a layover sample for potential clients. This was not about work, or publicity, or mileage... this was about her. If the other happened, she would have to count it as good luck and pure bonus.

Dan grabbed a mug and came and stood with her. He looked at her quickly and said, "Pensive? Or just annoyed?"

Was she really that obvious? "A little of both. They think it is a 'Reno'."

"Yeah, they don't get it... but we know," and in a moment his wink transported her irritation into an exquisite secret.

She smiled appreciatively. "Doesn't that drive you nuts?"

"Their lack of insight? Sure, but that's family for you." He grinned mischievously. "Guess it goes both ways. I probably don't get their stuff either, but perhaps they don't realise I haven't a clue, because I tend not to say much."

"Are you saying I talk too much?"

"Nope. Only speaking for myself."

"Oh boy, you are annoying. No one else follows these sorts of rules." She looked out the window.

"You okay?"

"Sure why?"

"There is just the slightest glassy glint in your eye that makes me suspect you want to hit something... really hard."

"Am I really so transparent? I thought I was being very good..."

"Oh yes. Maintaining the highest standards of best behaviour. I congratulate you."

"Huh. Are you worried about your windows?"

"I'd hate Smithy to come back from holidays and find a bigger mess than when he left."

Mac appreciated his attempt to keep it light-hearted. "So. How long have you been a preacher?"

He grinned. "Huh. Didn't really think I was. Thank you." And he nodded at the compliment.

"You know what I mean. Doing the religious thing."

"Hmm – different question I think."

"You are avoiding the issue. Tell me."

"Okay... question one. Been on the preaching roster since I came back here after Dad died. Don't do it very often, just sort of relief, mostly when Smithy is away. The religious question – can't be sure. Never really thought of myself as religious. Gave my heart to Jesus when I was about eight. Kinda hung in there with varying levels of commitment until I was in my late teens... had a bit of a crisis and needed to make a choice. I chose God... or He chose me. Not sure which. Since then, we've been pretty good mates. That's about it."

"Mates? Are you serious? How can you be mates with God? You don't look like that type at all." Friends. Huh. That was a reoccurring theme. And now with God?

"I didn't know it had a particular type."

She blinked and shook her head. The man was messing with her. He swung hammers for a living. And teenagers were supposed to be rebellious not religious. It didn't fit with her understanding of the way things worked. She thought about when she was nineteen. God was the last thing on her radar.

❧

Mac came up to the studio. It was not far off lock up and she did the tour, checking in. Today it felt like she was at work again, and she noticed a few things and addressed them. Once an oversight like that would have set her blood boiling. Deviations from the plan were not tolerated. But, well, now the ranting seemed unnecessary. It probably wasn't that big a deal. Besides she had to acknowledge that if she'd been more consistently present, something like this would never have got far. Still, it wasn't according to the plan, and she was one for sticking to the plan. And her plan for today involved plants. Lots of plants.

"Dan, I want to ask a favour. I'm going into Blackstone today to pick up an order from the nursery." She took a deep breath. "And... ahh... I was wondering if I could borrow your ute?"

"You want to borrow my ute?" Dan turned to her curiously and half closed his eyes as if it helped him process the question.

"I'm asking nicely... please. I can put more stuff in it than my car. I'll fuel it up of course. Should be back by four."

"Hmm?" He was enjoying her awkwardness as she humbly grovelled.

"Well?" She was peeved that he looked so smug about this.

Dan sent his offsider to unhook his trailer and empty the back tray of the accumulated stuff that had congregated there. He watched him go and then turned back to Mac. "I would just like to clarify the basis of this borrowing favour. Are we talking friend? Contractor? If it is as a contractor, I would feel obligated to charge a hire fee."

"You wouldn't!"

His eyes were teasing, in a relaxed sort of way. "Depends on the parameters I suppose. A fee wouldn't apply to a friend of course."

"If it is so inconvenient just say no. It's not a big deal."

"I don't want to say no. I want to understand..."

"Understand what?"

"The basis of your request: contractor, neighbour, bond-slave, friend?"

"You are determined to get me to say I consider you a friend, which I have no intention of doing. I have no idea why you think that is so important."

He looked at her. "Seriously, Stanzie? You have no idea?"

"Mac."

"Stanzie. If I am a good enough to lend you my ute as a friend; then I qualify friend enough to call you by name."

"My name is Mac."

"Your name is Constance Macintosh; shortened to Stanzie. That is personal."

"You have no idea what I consider personal!"

"Except every time you say it... or I say it, you blush. Believe me, its personal."

"Oh, all right. I'll say it. I would like to borrow your ute because I would rather not have the inconvenience of driving to Blackstone to pick up a hire vehicle. I'd have to then drive all the way back there to drop it off when I could take your ute and have it all done in half the time for half the cost. It is something one could normally ask of a friend, and perhaps I do consider that we know each other well enough to extend to that. There. Satisfied?"

"Nearly."

"Nearly? What else could you possibly want to wring out of this?"

"I want to call you by your name: Stanzie. Anytime. All the time."

"Why?"

"Because I think it is worth fighting for. You asked what extortion I would want. This is it. I want that."

"Huh. You're nuts. No way. Not happening."

Dan pulled out his keys and dangled them in front of her. "I could tell my mother you thought she was Methuselah incarnate."

She stared at him. "What the hell is a Methuselah?"

"The oldest dude in the Bible... he lived to 969 years old. Some trivia for you."

"You wouldn't tell Iris I thought that! That's just horrible!"

"I told you I would give you the fight of your life. Didn't say I would fight fair."

"This is the fight of my life?"

He shrugged. "It starts with a name. It's important to me. Besides I'm right. You're digging into the trenches: fighting."

"Well, I'm not convinced it is going to be helpful. Nope. I need to keep this professional."

He shrugged and put the keys back in his pocket. "Enjoy your trip to Blackstone," he said and turned and took his tape-measure off his belt.

"I can't believe you! You are so selfish!"

He shrugged. "That may be. But I am consistent. You want to be my friend and borrow my ute... the payoff is I get to call you by name, as a friend."

"You arrogant, stubborn... Uugh!!"

He shrugged. Unmoved. He made a measurement and marked it with a pencil.

"Okay!"

He looked up. "Okay?"

She nodded. Unimpressed.

He pulled out the keys, and placed them in her hand, holding them there for just a short pause. "Perhaps you need to work out why it sticks in your throat so much, Stanzie. Drive safe."

Damn it, he was right. She blushed.

For the forty-five minutes on the drive to Blackstone, no matter how loud the music was or how much she wanted to ignore it, his challenge taunted her. Why was she digging into the trenches? This couldn't be just about keeping it professional. Dan was capable and reputable. She doubted that he would suddenly become 'unprofessional' because of her name.

This name thing had been a bugbear all her life. "Stanzie..." her mum had said one day over a mug of hot milo bobbing with marshmallows, "You fight it. Well, I did too. I was so determined not to give in to your father about this. We brawled tooth and nail over your name. Constance: it sounds so musical. Reminds me of Mendelssohn, even though Constance was Mozart's wife. I even called one of Mendelssohn's 'Songs without Words' Constance... it seemed to fit so well next to his Consolation. You are amongst illustrious company, Stanzie..." Mum and her music. And Mac had rolled her eyes and thought, "But he hadn't actually called any of his compositions Constance and besides, they weren't drawings..." If it wasn't visual, it wasn't art, and it didn't count.

Funny, it was not until then, driving the ute into Blackstone, that she realised her dad had never, ever called her Constance. Nor had he shortened it to Stanzie. Not once. In his own typical passive-aggressive style, he had got his way. "C-C," he would say, "you've got too much spunk for that sort of namby-pamby romantic stuff. You're a do-er... just like your old man, hey? C-C and D-D. We're doers." What he actually did, Mac was never sure. But when he left, she had no doubt in her mind, he had gone to 'do' whatever spunky-real-stuff he did, and it was definitely not wishy-washy and definitely not dreamy. And she smirked at the timid revelation, that she had romanticised his leaving into some sort of idealistic mission to experience real-life: 'Doing' in all its totality. Perhaps this was why she found the landscaping so satisfying. It fitted her definition of *Doing*. Or her dad's. She turned into the nursery parking space and wondered why she would even think that. She pictured the very stark, plain, ugly yard of her childhood, because Mum didn't have the time, and Dad didn't have the energy.

When the nursery confirmed the arrival of her plants, she was more than ready to start adding them to the garden-beds freshly prepared with imported topsoil and mulch. She already had the pond liner, water feature, solar panelling, and pump. That old flutter of anticipation stirred in her belly as she thought about the space it would create.

Mac had refined shopping to a military manoeuvre. Rarely did she make a decision standing in a shop. Buying the fish on this excursion was no exception. She stared at the tank, all her notes on fish in her hand, and made an unemotional selection according to the size of her proposed pond. The assistant happily scooped them into four plastic bags and tied the top. It was only as she was driving home that she realised that her fish could end up as fertilizer if she didn't get their habitat sorted out very quickly. She chided herself for not considering her timeframes better. She reached over and patted the bags sitting on the front seat. "Sorry guys. You'll be home soon."

It was strong motivation to go straight to work, to at least get the basics installed. Fish. She liked the idea that they had this whole other world that people were rarely privy to: living in this microcosm of privacy. Who understood her private microcosm? Who knew her as she was, and not how she marketed herself? Who cared about her private little pond enough to ask how it was going? Her mum did. Had. Oh Mum... with all her old-fashioned eccentricities. Tears stung her eyes as she unloaded the plants. And then she went straight to work manoeuvring rocks and plastic, watched by the forlorn misshapen shape of the willow.

She had once heard a story where there was a pond that collected all the tears of a maiden and turned the water into an elixir that had healing powers. Where was her healing elixir? All she had was an empty hole by a willow tree that didn't look anything like her fishpond. She hated that she was struggling to create the arrangement as she saw it. It was not working. She kicked at the turned dirt and growled in frustration. More tears! This was her design. She was the artist, so she should be able to paint this on the canvas of her garden. Her hands-on plan was intended to lower stress levels, not escalate them. She sat under the tree, the pond-form frustratingly, tantalizingly close, but not close enough... and she cried and cried.

Mum. Mum would say something wise and annoying and hit the nail on the head. Without her here, everything seemed wrong. Her ugly reality was that she was alone... alone as they come. She didn't even know how to change that. The inertia was strangling her. She needed motion. She craved it. "Oh God. It's like I'm paralysed..." and a moan escaped her lips coming from a deep part in her chest.

She wanted to rise up in independent competence and be the kind of woman she so admired: just like she was before. The strong one, who didn't need others, but graciously, condescendingly allowed them entry. Stanzie had sat with her Mum one evening on the day-chaise.

"Stanzie, I can't blame God for this... and I don't want you to, either. He loves me... and that is stronger than the pain." Stanzie had just got up and made up some more tea. How could Mum trust God in this! The pain was so bad it made her whimper in her bed when she thought Stanzie was asleep. Wasn't that the ultimate betrayal? She had been a good person! She didn't deserve that!

The sun was dipping low, and coolness started to creep along the ground. Now Stanzie wondered if there was, in fact, something worse than the pain. Somehow the stillness responded to an unasked question in her chest. What if aloneness was worse? There was no choice in the rough, unbidden road her mum had to travel. Yet still she insisted that she had one significant option left: she chose to be with God while she walked her designated path. "We'll get through this Stanzie. We will. Together." Stanzie knew full well she had been talking mostly about God responding to that awful aloneness in her. But it didn't seem like she got through it at all. In the end she died... horribly. Stanzie took off her gloves, pulled a tissue from her pocket and blew her nose. How could her mum believe that not-alone was enough? A resounding silence answered her pondering.

"Am I disturbing you?" Stanzie jolted, a look of horror washing over her face. Dan stepped back.

"Are you okay?" he asked quietly.

"I... you startled me, that's all."

"Ah-huh. I got held up, but I'm here now."

Oh, my goodness. She could have sworn he was he inside her head! Heavens. She was getting herself in a flap! That was something else her mother would say.

Dan looked into her face. "Something's got you worked up..." He raised his eyebrow, just slightly.

Stanzie rubbed her forehead, leaving a dirty smudge. She wondered if she could... would... level with him. "No. You're right..." She coughed and covered her embarrassment by getting philosophical. "I can always see my designs. I know what they are supposed to be and when they are converted from here," she touched her forehead again, "to there." She swept her hand over her attempt at rocks and pond-liner. "But this is totally wrong! It isn't translating at all. I should be able to get it from here to there. I'm the artist; this is what I do! I feel like I'm starting to lose it!"

"Well, you could be in luck. I'm a translator. That's what I do."

Stanzie stared at the billowing clouds, glowing around the fringes as the last remaining twilight started to darken. Metaphorical silver linings. It privately astounded her that she didn't doubt that Dan could do what he claimed. In fact, she knew he could. But his help was not at all like her picture of "Independent Girl" with a star-trimmed cape. She sat silently for a moment and considered the possibility of letting him in. Yes, she could, as terrifying as that was. She became aware how the inertia inside her, just slightly, started to shift. In one way it felt quite surreal, and in another way, it felt as normal as anything. And she didn't understand how those two dimensions could even coexist side by side.

22.

Dan sat at her table looking curiously at the growing collection of art supplies dumped there. This didn't fit with his picture of the ordered architect he had contracted to work with, and he was curious at this another side of her. He twisted his neck to look at a stray sketch discarded on top of some papers. He picked it up, and then looked at another lying on the table under a tray of pastels. He compared it to a canvas, already marked out, set on an easel beside the window. She was gifted. No doubt about it.

He wondered how long it took a girl to have a camp shower. Finally, he got up and washed up a coffee cup and flicked on the electric jug. He sat down again, mug in hand and looked at some other sketches. He considered a series of silhouettes: the willow, stark in its bare autumn exposure against the setting sky. He lingered over another: a pond... sparkling beside the old willow. Unbelievable. This is what she saw. And as he looked at it, he understood her frustration, and what needed to be done to create that mesmerizing sense of balance. Symmetry.

He had assumed artists found something already there, that captured their attention to portray on canvas. But Stanzie seemed to find something that captured her imagination and then created it, so it could arrest someone else's attention. So back to front. So unexpected. So extraordinarily interesting.

162

He heard her rattling at the door as she came in towelling her hair dry. "Sorry. Takes a while..."

Her wet hair looked dark against the backlight of the doorway and there was something quite disarming in that domestic, familiar act of wrapping a towel turban around her head that made him swallow. Trying very hard to appear nonchalant, he shrugged and held up the coffee mug. "I helped myself..."

"I was going to have a bite to eat. Did you want something? I have beef, lamb, vegetarian or chicken. No obligation to stay to the very last mouthful of course." She wondered if they could get through a meal without disagreeing or him leaving. Although, as if noticing for the first time, she observed they did do lunch together quite regularly now. She rummaged in her freezer. "Are you eating?"

"Sure. Mum's doing a beef phase, so chicken would be good."

"So many choices. I'm up for lamb. It is so nice not having to think about preparing food when I come in. I give your Mum something for the ingredients when I run low. I've always got a selection on standby. Freeze them in single serves. See... we did find a solution to the food dilemma. Now I feel totally spoilt rather than invaded. How hungry are you? One, two or three serves?"

"Two. Thanks." Was this really as normal, and as comfortable, as it sounded?

"I'm not talking work until after dinner... so don't ask." She handed him another coffee. She wondered if it really might be possible to talk about something rather than their common contact point. Could there ever be anything between them other than a studio apartment construction job?

"Sounds good to me."

"Really? I thought that might frustrate you."

"Why do you always assume the worst reactions from me? I haven't given you any reason to think that."

She laughed. "Oh right. Except the President of the Clean-Plate Republic abandoned food so he could make a point."

"Okay, I confess. Once. I felt cornered. I had to leave."

"Twice. And I thought you didn't feel obliged to do anything."

"I appreciate the vote."

The microwaved beeped and Stanzie got up. "What have you been looking at?"

"Your drawings," he said. "Found one of the fishpond. And at the risk of sounding like I'm talking shop, I get what you are trying to do. It is really very well composed."

"Well, don't sound so surprised. But that's the easy part. Now I have to do it."

"Why is it so urgent that *you* have to do it? You created this. Does it really matter if someone else puts it together? Of all your awards, how much of the design did you construct? You still got the credit."

"But I wanted to do this one myself. I don't want help."

"Yeah, you do. You want help so bad you are paying for it."

"Except that if I pay, it's not help; it's business."

"Oh. So business is not helpful? How can it only be help if it's free, if it's charity? That's nuts."

Stanzie jolted and looked away. Oh, he knew how to unnerve her. "Business is safer, that's all. I want to do this myself," she repeated.

He grinned. "There it is again: Little Red Hen."

"Ahh, well, Little Red Hen had to do it all herself. She was one of my childhood heroes."

"The Little Red Hen is your idea of a heroine? What happened to Tinkerbelle or Wonder-woman?"

"That story was very motivating. My mum had this very romantic notion of choosing some of the less common fables and telling them to music. Thumbelina was another one. Rumpelstiltskin got a beating over how the Miller's boasting jeopardised his family. She'd sit at the piano and tell the story. The Little Red Hen plodding over to the pigpen, or to the cow yard to ask for help. The sunshine and the rain that fell on the paddock the Little Red Hen ploughed. It's weird, but I could smell the rain on those freshly ploughed paddocks in her music. It was like our own personal soundtrack. I could feel the sunshine on my face and see the seeds sprouting..."

"Wow! What an incredible childhood memory. That's an inspiring way to tell a story!!"

"It was. It has become embedded in Macintosh folklore: do it yourself."

"So, this becomes your rationale for ruthless independence? I always thought the point of the story was about the others not getting to enjoy the rewards without contributing. She wanted help but no one was willing..." He swallowed again and looked away. "Guess you are in luck Little Red Hen: I'm willing to give you a hand." Did he just say that? God, am I really at the 'giving' part? Has my 'want-to' changed so thoroughly?

"Yeah, well, that's where the story and I part ways. I don't want help. Nothing personal: it's not just your help: it's any help. I need to do this on my own. This is supposed to be my therapy."

"Which part is the therapy?"

"Well, the doing part of course."

"And what aren't you doing?"

"Well... the building for a start. I quit on that." She got up and stirred the meals again.

"Quit? I thought you delegated."

"Humph." Why was he always trying to make it sound better than it was? She much preferred calling it like it is...

which amounted to failing to meet her own tough, uncompromising expectations, time after time.

Dan looked thoughtfully at the sketch in his hand. "If I was asked to design something like this I'd break out in a cold sweat. I can draft up a fair design and might get close to it in the end... but the process would have me stressed and strung out." She didn't say anything. "If 'Doing' looked the same for everyone, the job would never get done."

Well, she could acknowledge that. "Guess I've always regarded 'Doing' as the less deskbound aspects of the job."

"Deskbound? You're constantly on the job. And the landscaping... you can't get more involved than that. Give yourself a break. What you're 'doing' is not quitting or deskbound."

She shook her head. Why was he so insistent on defending her? It was unnerving that she couldn't be defensive with him.

Dan smirked. "I don't think you could be deskbound. That's what makes you good. Checking the translation is accurate at every stage. You've found stuff I've missed..."

It started to rain. Stanzie stared out the window into the dark. "I think I need my arbour built. I don't like the idea of my bench-seat out in the weather."

"Fishpond, arbour, studio apartment. You need all sorts of help... of both the business and charitable kind." He had to just accept the fact that this job was no longer just business. It was personal. God. Can this possibly go anywhere? Even if it doesn't, am I still willing to help? Yep. He had arrived at that place. Inconveniently, that was exactly where he was. Damn. Inconveniently damn.

❧⌘❧

After Dan finished up at the studio the next day, he found Stanzie by the pond. "Thought you said you'd work elsewhere, and we'd look at this together?" he said.

"I have been doing other stuff. But this is driving me nuts."

"It's fixable. It'll be okay."

"I don't understand why. I designed it; I should be able to get it right."

"Well, I'm kinda relieved. Otherwise, I would be of no use to you at all."

"Huh. I believe our first argument was about you feeling used."

"Touché." Dan started stripping the pond-site back, removing stones. Stanzie pitched in. He stared at her then. Seeing her gloved and dirty... lugging rocks from here to there. It was very different to her sitting opposite him at the servo with her ruffled hair, sipping her coffee, trying hard to make a strong business impression. Something had changed. She was beautiful.

She looked up and saw him watching her. "What?"

He nodded. "You're alright, Stanzie Macintosh," he said with approval as she stacked more rocks to one side.

"Doesn't feel like it. Being independent would be easier."

"So, it's established that the Little Red Hen doesn't like charity."

Stanzie jumped. He was turned away and she was thankful he didn't notice... or did he? "I believe I said independent."

"Which I took to mean... not being charitable. See I'm right. Charity," He grinned. "Charity, charity. Sounds a like a train: charity-charity-charity. Why can't it be a locomotive that lightens the load? Charity, charity..."

"Enough already! Goodness, you know how to go on."

His grin faded as he looked at her and handed her a shovel. "Guess the point about charity, is that nothing is owed: it's free. Still, if you like... let's just agree that while we're doing this, we'll keep it square. Fifty-fifty. No bottom line. Just two friends mucking in a pond together... like pigs."

"Gross. That is a very unattractive picture."

"My forebears used to run pigs on this block. A point of industry that some in my family found particularly humiliating, I think." He pulled out the plastic liner and flicked it, and it sent a shower of dirt over her as she turned away. It spilled down the back of her collar, clinging through her hair.

"What the..." She spluttered and swore, as she tried to shake the dirt from down her shirt.

"Sorry."

"You are not!" She took the shovel in her hand and tossed a pile of dirt over his chest.

He laughed at her. "Fifty-fifty. See, you're good at this game. So, are we agreed? No charity. Just even. Are you up for that?"

She frowned. He was not at all upset by her vengeful comeback. "Okay. You give it; I'll give it back. And vice-versa. That way we're square."

"Sounds fair. Whatever 'it' is."

"I can keep up. No problem. Dirt for dirt; rock for rock; loan for loan; acknowledgment, insult or compliment," she said.

"The ultimate Dutch-date."

"Dutch it maybe. Date? I don't think so."

"Could be. I owe you a meal from last night. You said so yourself. Meal for meal." Dan started to scrape the bottom of the pond with the shovel. He focused hard on what he was doing and tried not to look at her.

"Caught in a web of my own devising."

He grinned. "Perfect. Saturday. Lunch. I'll pick you up."

"Don't look so pleased. Can't do lunch: I'll be working. Sorry."

"Okay then: Dinner. After work. Dinner for dinner. That's even better. Six o'clock. I'll still pick you up, but we'll take your car. In exchange for the ute. All square."

"Where are we going?"

He shrugged. "You wouldn't want to spoil all my fun," he said. He had absolutely no idea.

23.

He arrived at six in his best jeans. He had no idea what she would expect or not expect. She opened the donga door also in jeans, heels and a sleeveless top that sparkled in the lamplight behind her. Guess she figured that there would be nothing in the area that this would not cater to. Dan felt relieved he had made the reservation in Blackstone.

Certainly not the classiest venue he'd ever taken a girl, but a step up from Gumleigh Pub.

He paused at the door of her car. "Would you mind if I drive? Since I know where we are going, and you don't."

Stanzie shrugged and handed him the keys. "Why not?"

When he turned onto the road towards Blackstone, Dan responded to her raised eyebrows and dubious look. "Fifty-fifty. You took the ute to Blackstone; so, we are going to Blackstone." And he grinned just a tad when he saw her go to object, and then close her mouth. Twice.

Dinner was unremarkable. No gross inefficiencies from the wait-staff; the food was conventional but acceptable. Dan was relieved and Stanzie benignly reserved. As they left, Dan opened the car door and paused. "One detour before we go home?"

She shrugged. "Sure." It was not like she had anywhere else to be. Her calendar was wide open at the moment.

172

He smiled. "Dinner and a show." He took her along a back country road and turned off onto gravel that stopped at a dead-end where he parked. "We walk from here..."

"Really – you want me to go bush walking in the middle of the night... in heels? I could break something."

"No doubt. We'll go slowly. It's not far... and you can hang onto me," he added as an afterthought. He took out his phone and flicked on the torch feature. She could hear a creek running over rocks and some birds called out, echoing around the dark cathedral chambers of the night forest.

"You're not taking me out here to dispose of me, are you?"

"I could think of more convenient places if that was what I had in mind. Careful... we step down. Here, hold my phone." He jumped down and lifted her lightly to his side. She stumbled slightly into his arms, and he braced her firmly, pausing. She didn't move for just a moment.

"Greif! This is painstaking. Is it going to be worth the effort?"

He wondered in which eon of time-travel she would ever allow 'romantic'. Perhaps gold spinning for Rumpelstiltskin was more likely since that was also one of her favourite childhood stories. Dan chuckled. Well not tonight apparently. He guided her into an overhanging cavern and switched off his torch. "We're here."

"Here? Well, this is fun. We just sit in the dark?"

"That's the idea. What do you see?"

"It's pitch black, you idiot. I can't see a thing." He laughed at her. "Let your eyes adjust a bit."

"I can see a couple stars outside... there... maybe."

"Uhuh. Anything inside?"

"Nup. What is your point?"

"Well, I didn't actually have a point. Just thought you might enjoy this. But if I was to use this moment to make a life-lesson from... it could be that everything is not necessarily explained by previous experience. It might be something new, unexpected, and beautiful."

"So, we are looking for interesting? Okay. Now I'm assuming I'm not getting it. Like... what?"

He paused and gently leaned over and held her arm towards a faint glimmer. "Like... glow-worms."

"Oh," she said in a whisper, "No way!" She sat still for a moment. "Like May Gibbs'? Glow worms? Is that...?" Her voice reverently hushed as she looked up and around her becoming aware of the iridescent clusters of glow-worms lighting the roof of the cavern. "I love May Gibbs. Her work was my favourite growing-up... so amazing." They sat reverently for a long time as more lights turned on. "Oh wow. Bush Christmas-lights..." she said in hushed tones.

"See over there... a fire-fly. Blinking around the trees over by the creek..."

"I thought Gibbs just invented fire-flies to accommodate the lack of electricity in her Australian bush world, along with whimsical gum-nut babies, and scary banksia men. Is it really blinking?"

"I think so... strobing. Plain little bugs with backsides that glow. Kind of interesting..."

"I believe you are on a mission to uncover a whole world for me that is more than it seems. Do you know I even look at the underside of mushrooms now?" Dan was interested; she sensed that. But would he ever find her interesting... by his own definition? That would be so irresistible, so desirable, so breath-taking.

24.

Was she game?   Stanzie pulled the box out from under the woollen throw and put aside all the other stuff she had piled on top to keep it out of sight. She sat on the lounge and glared at it. What was the worst thing opening it could mean? Was it possible to be any more disillusioned than she already was? What if there was evidence of another family? Another love? What if it wasn't that he didn't want to do family; he just didn't want to do family with them? She read stories like that. What if this became her story? She felt her anger mounting.

She got up and walked around. Perhaps she should not do this alone. She came back and sat in front of it. Quickly, she went to the kitchen and pulled out a roll of garbage bags. One to give to the Salvo's. The other to dump. Maybe another to keep.

Stanzie grabbed at the tape and yanked it off, tearing the flimsy cardboard off in shreds. She pulled back the flaps, then sat and stared. Really. She felt like she needed tongs; forceps to prevent cross-contamination. There was a dirty cheap cap; an unwashed, smelly t-shirt. How humiliating. A saucepan with a burnt bottom and a gas-burner; a packet of cigarettes, and a lighter. Shame filled her, embarrassed by the depth of failure. She shook her head unable to comprehend why a landlady would think any of this stuff could be of interest to anybody, kin or otherwise. Perhaps it was just the convenience of shoving it over for someone else to deal with. She sighed. Next of kin. Huh. This was her heritage? Not likely. She didn't want to own this. Yet there still remained a whisper of that unspoken desire to see the man underneath the grime and cheapness. Was there anything redeemed or redeemable? What was left of the artist her mother fell in love with? Or the dad she so passionately defended? Why had her emotional pendulum swung so dramatically to the other side? It probably wouldn't matter if she unearthed an ancient golden artefact of great significance. He would stand condemned for heathen idol worship. Just something else added to his list of crimes.

She continued through the accumulation of meaningless junk. A cheap paper-back western; a near empty bottle of cheap scotch; a musty, thread-bare towel; a couple of letters of demand. It all went in the garbage bag. Then she retrieved the demand letters and wondered if she would take responsibility for this too. More stuff. In the bag. This was seriously hard. Had he been so utterly isolated and disenfranchised that this was all he had left of his microcosm... his fishpond? The world that he so desperately wanted to expand was ultimately so very, very small.

She held his wallet for a moment; worn and tattered – it looked like something that had been with him for decades. She shuffled through it – an expired driver's licence. She considered his photo, which seemed more like a mugshot, awkward and dull. She put the license on the table. This was the most recent photo she had of him, and she felt vaguely disappointed that this was not a case of mistaken identity. It really was Donny. What picture was all this stuff painting for her? Receipts from a Seven-Eleven convenience store and a Bottle-Mart. Rice. He ate rice. Hardly a very complete picture of the man behind the box. What else? There was nothing in the second-hand recyclable bag. It had all gone in the dump-bag.

Right at the bottom of the carton was an old shoe box. She opened it. There were envelopes – some in her mother's handwriting. She cautiously turned them over... and then opened them up, one by one and laid them out chronologically. Her mother had spent a lot of time writing about his daughter's schooling, her art, her netball, her dance-classes. The requests for money stopped and were replaced by declines to send him funds. She could read the frustration in her mother's hand. "Donny," she wrote, "Stanzie needs new shoes, new swimmers, school books. You should be providing for her, not be asking for money from your own daughter!" It sounded way too civilized for Stanzie's liking. She could think of a million ways to say that in vernacular he might understand. But that was her Mum. Gentle, trodden on, worn, and kind. Even in the face of cruel. The letters stopped the year she turned fifteen. She found some other envelopes from her mum. Stanzie's drawings still folded inside, unnoticed; newspaper clippings, evidently unread; photographs, disregarded. Perhaps she had hoped to find pin-marks or blue-tac stains: evidence of a wall of honour, like those TV episodes where the father secretly follows a child's life, turning up incognito to awards nights and sporting carnivals. She often scanned the sea of faces and wondered if one of those set of eyes belonged to Dad, proudly leaning over to his neighbour saying, "That's my girl…"

When Stanzie opened the envelope of the cat drawing, it was like she had landed in a pit filled with a seething morass of venomous snakes: something out of an Indiana Jones adventure. The thing you hate most is the thing you are confronted with. She finally felt compelled to admit it. It was unlikely that this fantasy of hers even remotely resembled her dad's version of parenting. The idea of family offered him nothing. No satisfaction. No glow of pride… and he had offered nothing in return.

Stanzie sat there on her lounge and held the drawing that all these years had been her heart-connection with her dad. As she held it, she realised it was weathered by time but not worn from handling. It seemed likely he never looked at – at least not for long. She imagined him checking the envelope for money and when no cheque fell out, stashed it away in this box of useless memorabilia. Only one consolation remained: he had stashed it, and not binned it.

❧ഇരു❧

For days that empty box stood untouched. Even if this aloneness was his preference, what right did he have to impose it on her? Not only had she lost a connection-point with her father, but this man had also died lonely and alone. It would have been pathetic and sad if she was not so angry. How completely selfish that he would choose this! He had his choices. Eight-year-old Stanzie had none. None at all. And that was not fair!

Stanzie didn't want to allow that any of this was his choice. What if it was beyond him? Outside his control? Did she have any right to condemn that? She would never know. She wished it was different, but she knew it was not, and never would be. The ugly truth was that at some point he chose isolation, and his life was poorer because of the direction he trod. Something in him did not have the capacity to stay, and she would never know why that was.

As she looked at the bottom of the empty carton, she realised she had been hoping for one sample of his work, but there was no drawing in the box that had been his. The artist that her father had been remained a mystery. Nothing in this carton provided an explanation behind his poverty and isolation. Perhaps it wasn't like that at all. Perhaps he was content. Introverts sometimes are. Yet this box did not provide evidence of contentment. Just aloneness. She pulled her art-pad onto her knee and into that loneliness she started to draw. A portrait of a lonely old man, twisted and tortured by the forces of his environment and weather, becoming something that no one admired, no one cared for... no one desired. Alone and bent. Ugly and wild. A willow of a man. And yet in that unattractive and embarrassing form there was some aspect of it that somehow drew her attention back to it, again and again. Something that reminded her of her own frailty, her own vulnerability, her own flaws, her own ugly... and as she shaded the scars along that tortured aged skin, Stanzie found that she could acknowledge she was not to blame. The way he was, she knew now, was not their fault. She could concede his choices hurt and wounded. She could allow that life is not fair. She recognised that the whole thing stank of cheap gin, grief, and pain, and she no longer hated him; she pitied him. Perhaps in time, she wondered if that also might change... into accepting him for who he was. Perhaps... but not yet. For now... as she shaded along the shadows of this stranger, she allowed her own dark resentment to recede and merge and release. Tears spilt onto the page, blurring the coarseness of that texture where they fell. "Dad, you bastard!" She knew her mother forgave him long ago. How desperately Stanzie wanted her mother to be wrong. She wanted to believe his hand was forced. She thought that if he hadn't wanted to go, that made it better; that there would be no crime to forgive. But pain is its own crime, and this was a crime committed against her mother... and against her. She recalled how many tears her mother had cried over that hurt. Stanzie had finally had enough of the stoic, grim façade. Now it was her time to cry. He had broken her heart... not just by being weak. He was also cruel. "In time I might be able to think of this differently. This is it for now." She laid her hand on her drawing like a benediction... and whispered, "Dad. I hope you find the peace in eternity, that you didn't find here." And she cried into the cushion she hugged in her lap, the grief of an eight-year-old girl who never understood.

25.

Stanzie was determined she wasn't going to be outdone by Dan's dinner and show. Fifty-fifty. But what? She could take him to a stage play, but surround-sound and theatrical glamour didn't seem to be quite on the same transcendent level as glow-worms in a bush cavern. Something less pretentious, like a movie? Something personal? Should it be original, something he hadn't already seen? If he had already done it, would he do it again? She didn't want to put herself out there and have him despise her offering.

She was down by the fishpond, tidying up around the water's edge, adjusting rocks, digging soil and planting. It was looking beautiful; slightly bare, but the area had come together in every way, just as she had wanted. She glued two little plagues on stones near the little cascading water feature, 'In Memory', with the names Shirley and Donny on one: Dave, Alex and Toni on the other. It seemed like a gesture that gave substance to the work that was done here... and not just the landscaping.

She loved the idea that this canvas would be relentlessly changing... growing, maturing. Nothing would stay the same. It couldn't. Once she would have found that frustrating. A building, when it is constructed is set, stable, unchanging... except for the effects of age. That was what she had appreciated about her work; it was a mark she had left on the world. She wondered if her career sat so well, because construction seemed constant, a bit like herself: Constance. And yet Constance was never a name she associated with work. And it was only now, while working on something that was by its very nature changing and changeable, that her name seemed to fit better. What was that about?

She found herself checking her watch. She mentioned to Dan that she was releasing her fish into the pond this afternoon. He hadn't seemed insulted by the idea, so just before four, she went up to the studio and grabbed the temporary tubs that held her fish. Dan was stacking away tools. "Hey, I've got something in the ute when you add your fish. Nearly done here."

He drove down to the pond and then produced a basket and blanket. "You seem to like the idea of marking an occasion with a little bit of ceremony. The coming home of your new family members seems like a suitably important event."

She looked at him to see if he was having a go at her, but his eyes were clear and sincere, and he dragged a large, shaped metal mesh sheet from the back of his ute. "What's this?" said Stanzie hesitantly as she lifted out her tubs of fish. Her temporary fish-tanks had taken its toll and she was relieved to be finally putting them in the pond.

"Security. The kookaburras will love you for serving up fresh fish so conveniently for them: king of the kingfishers.

But you won't have a guppy left to your name in three days if we don't do something to curtail their enthusiasm. This mesh is fine enough to do the job. I've left lugs so it'll sit just under the surface. It shouldn't be too noticeable once your water-lilies get going. They'll have somewhere to hide."

Hmm. Why did 'sensible' always sound like a compromise on 'attractive'? But she had no desire to have her progeny served as a fresh-food smorgasbord. "So, now for the ceremonial releasing of the fish. May your days be long, fertile, playful, and safe," she said gently in a benediction, submerging the buckets and tipping them forward so they could swim out.

Dan grinned and watched them swim away exploring their new home. He secured the mesh and poked through some of the water plants and reeds. Stanzie flicked open the picnic rug and sat, peeking in the basket to find what Iris had packed for their little afternoon tea. Jam tarts and little chocolate pastry mushrooms. Mushrooms. Interesting. Now he had her on two accounts: a show and a picnic. "Are you doing anything next Saturday?" she said casually.

"Don't think so..." He tried to sound nonchalant, but it came across dubious. He handed her a drink, and she popped the can as he sat down beside her.

"Oh. Well, if you are busy... that's okay. However, on the basis of fifty-fifty, I now owe you a show and a picnic. I... well, I have an inclination to go painting outdoors... and I wondered if you knew a spot. I could rustle up a picnic..."

"So, what's the 'show' part?"

"Nothing as cool as glow-worms and fire-flies, but I've haven't painted outdoors since art classes a long time ago... so you should appreciate the gesture, because I will be way outside my comfort zone, and it will never happen again. You can watch or do whatever catches your fancy. Read a book."

He grinned. "Don't think you'll let me do what catches my fancy. I'll bring a book."

She flushed. Oh, my goodness, he was flirting with her. Definitely interested.

"So. What do you want to paint? Mountains, trees, creeks... what outdoorsy place are you after?" he asked.

"Hmm... always the architect. I was really hoping for an old farmhouse... a bit like this before we started. A shed maybe. Something old and run-down. Anything like that around? I'll probably just end up painting my place, but it may offer inspiration and atmosphere."

"Ahh. Possibly have something in mind."

A kookaburra burst out laughing. Stanzie jolted and looked around cautiously. She'd never thought of their mirth as sinister before. She really liked her fish. She wanted their microcosm world to be a safe place.

❧•ଽଆ•❧

Stanzie parked the work ute and let Frank-L out to run around. Dan had insisted that her low convertible would not cope with the terrain. The track had been overgrown with tall brown grass blowing in sweeping waves up the hill. The house stood on the crest with its wide verandahs, collapsing roofline and smashed windows. A couple of elegant Jacaranda trees stood gracefully by, defying the ravaged destruction they witnessed year in, year out. There was a sad aura about her, grandly standing there like a rickety old lady trying vainly to retain her dignity.

Stanzie got out and stood before her, silently saluting her charm, her past, her design. There was something poignant about her bygone grandeur. Perhaps there was an echo of one removalist carton sitting empty in her loungeroom that once belonged to a passionate artist and now only held the ruins of a disused existence. "Someone once loved you very much..." she whispered.

Dan said nothing, but came and stood with her, watching. He wondered what was going on in her heart. She was obviously moved. He felt gratified that he had met the brief; fascinated that this was the artist, not the project manager that he was meeting in this moment.

She walked around, looking at angles and perspectives and quirky little things that made homes unique. All the window latches had long been pilfered, but she could tell from the shape of the imprint left, the style they would have been, glittering brass to compliment the coloured glass. This had been quite a place. She could see this as it had been, with people, and friends and family... and an incredible feeling of sadness swept over her.

Finally, she came back and turned to Dan. "Thank you. Thank you for allowing me these impressions. This is such a gem. She is a beautiful old lady. Want to know what I see?" She retraced her steps... pointing out the line of the roof; the views captured from the sweep of the verandah and the focus of the windows and the missing latches. She took photos and close-ups and wide-angle shots.

He stared at her amazed. "I look at this and all I see is a has-been. Problems. And a bulldozer. There was a local group trying to get it heritage listed at one point, but it never got off the ground. If you could... what would you do with it? Could anything be done? Like Guthrie's Road... what would you do?"

"If this became a commission? Hmm. Well, obviously function determines form... but whether it was residential or otherwise, the feature of this place is the views. They've focused on the windows and verandah. So, I'd want to recapture that. Sweeping lines to reflect sweeping views. You're right about the bulldozer... too far gone to renovate. But I would want to keep something. The window frames perhaps. They are all silky oak. Some of the timbers. Perhaps replicate some of those decorative brackets and barge-trims. The chimney would make an unusual feature for an outdoor entertaining area... backdrop for the bar maybe... a courtyard could be extended out here overlooking this aspect there.

The views are incredible! I'd keep that feeling of heritage, the romantic, nostalgic. You know, it would make a great function venue. They could hire for the event... and have accommodation suites on that side. I'd love to get married here. Every aspect gets a view. There. That's what I'd do."

"Do you have someone in mind?"

"What for?"

"...to marry?"

She looked at him and laughed. "You're fishing."

"And...?"

She shook her head. "There's no fun if I take the bait straight away. No sport in that at all."

"But I am curious. You're a talented, attractive professional woman with annoying, pedantic habits and control issues. Surely someone is smitten with this combination." Yep. Getting close to the mark there.

"Right back at you Dan. I don't see a ring on your finger."

He held up his left hand. "Do you want to know?" She had wondered that he had no wedding ring. Divorced? He had never even really hit on her. That was odd. Was he gay? Or a monk? She raised an eyebrow and nodded. Yep. She did want to know.

He had been preparing himself for this: endless internal rehearsals. "When I was about nineteen, I fell madly in love with a redhead. She was stunning. Clever. And as wild as the colour of her hair. Every cliché and stereotype you can think of... Gillian was all of them. And she could not have found a more willing participant. We tore down a very reckless path and left a lot of destruction in our wake..."

He faltered, but continued, his voice rasping. "Everything about our relationship contradicted how I was raised... but I really believed that was what I wanted.

Gilly died after we'd been together about six months.

What struck me most was that it could have been... well, it should have been me. It was one of those defining existential wake-up calls. It frightened the hell out of me."

"Oh... I'm sorry..."

"So... the outcome was... since then, I've been very careful not to start something I didn't want to finish. And I'm here, looking at another person who is stunning and clever and talented and smart, yet who is not hell-bent on destruction, but on creation... and I confess, it has me interested. And I'm wondering... if there is any one..." His voice croaked awkwardly, and he swallowed hard.

"Nope. No one in mind. Just the idea of it." She thought her voice sounded clipped and flippant after what he had just said. It was too personal... too close. He swallowed again and then shrugged, grateful that she covered his emotion rather than highlighting it. He cleared his throat again and turned back to the ute. "That works for me then. Where would you like your picnic? This is your dinner-and-show."

"Over there under the Jacarandas. We can pretend we are sitting in white cane furniture, sipping cocktails, looking out at this magnificent 'panoramic vista'."

He turned back to her and his eyes smiled. "Interesting choice."

That little foray into honesty had Stanzie wondering. A momentary glimpse into a life that was not as sanitised as Dan Henry seemed. She wondered if she should have fabricated the identity of some other interested party... enough to keep distance. But then honesty deserved an honest answer: fifty-fifty.

After lunch she positioned her easel in full view of the house and painted to her heart's content. Dan had brought a book, but it lay beside him unopened. She painted into the dusk.

❧❦❧

191

26.

The back garden continued to develop as the studio progressed. Rock walls were marked out; drainage installed, footings poured, additional stones imported from the local quarry. The stonemason, Ernie, had his nephew with him: Jay, a young man with a tentative stutter. He was apprenticed recently and keen as mustard to please. Stanzie was determined to keep hands-on and negotiated a discount based on her hours of labouring. Neither of them said much; speech was particularly awkward for Jay, and the silence suited Stanzie well enough. It was a jigsaw in stone. They developed a system where they'd sort the stone into piles so they could anticipate which suitable size and shape of rock Ernie would need. Stanzie felt their progress was developing a steady rhythm. Ernie was big guy who never smiled, but once on a smoko break, he prodded Jay and said, "Never thought I'd be saying it, but we just might keep her on. Making good time."

Every so often Ernie would get his apprentice to make the placement of stone, and Jay would painstakingly test four or five options before he found one that worked for him. At those times Stanzie paced up to the studio and back so she didn't have to watch him spread the mortar, re-position the stone or tap it into place a hundred times. Honestly. More than once, she was on the verge of demanding the mason continue the job she had quoted for, but something restrained her. Perhaps it was the vision of a little girl looking at the mailbox, waiting for an affirmation that never came. She could give him this. Well, she needed the break anyway, and tolerated his slowness in the name of a rotation. Jay's confidence grew, and so did his work.

⚜

It was just an innocuous envelope. She opened it up and unfolded an invoice. She stared at it in disbelief. She rang Carl straight away. "Since when did we bill each other consultancy fees?"

Carl stammered and cleared his throat. "Mac, I've no idea what you are talking about. I didn't bill anything down to you."

"Well, I have an invoice here... in black and white, for landscaping consultancy fees. That's you Carl."

There was a pause and then, "Oh."

"Yeah, 'Oh'. What's it about?"

"Reg's been on this thing. A witch-hunt really. But I never even told anyone we've been talking. And we were just talking. It didn't go down anywhere."

"So, you reckon he's been screening correspondence? Tommy wouldn't authorise that sort of access."

"Perhaps he did. Reg's been snooping around in-trays. I printed out some options. Maybe he saw those.

Going on in Tommy's ear about pilfering work-time and such."

She swore. "I am not paying this. I work there! Put me through to Tommy!"

Carl cleared his throat again. "Um, Mac. Tommy's not here this week. Taken some time to go out to his shack. No reception up there either, you know. Reg's in charge while he's away."

"Reg? Well, isn't he a charmer? Timing is impeccable. Oh, my goodness; can it get any worse?" She threw it all in the bin. "Leave a message for Tommy, will you? I'll talk to him when he gets back."

But when the phone rang with the office number coming up on the screen, it was Reg. "I had a message to call you Mac."

"No, you didn't. I left a message for Tommy to call me when he gets back."

"Tommy's not in the office at the moment. He's asked me to handle things for him while he is away... which I'm doing."

"How enormously generous of you Reg. Gold stars for you. It's not urgent. I'll talk to Tommy when he returns."

"If it's about your invoice, I would like to draw your attention to the terms at the bottom of the page. If these are not met the matter will be handed over to a debt collector."

"You've got to be kidding me! You've way over-stepped the mark here! You are not my boss. I have precedence on my side. No one has ever invoiced in-house services between team members before."

"No, it seems not. It is about time."

"About time! Tommy's only proviso has been that it doesn't interfere with client work. There was no notification the rules had changed. This is just another of your try-hard attempts to win points. Pretty certain the only thing you're winning here is a fairly solid enemy."

"Hmm. Not scared. Anything done on work time automatically encroaches on client service. We are doing the right thing by the firm."

"Given that any business is the people within it, doing the right thing by people is the right thing. There is nothing to be gained, except your over-sized ego gets a chance to strut its stuff."

"You are pretty fortunate if you can be so dismissive of that sort of money... and its money that belongs to the firm. You have been misappropriating company resources Mac. Tut-tut."

"Oh, my goodness! You have a hide. You're the one who is out the door at 5:06 every afternoon. I have given over and above, more than you could possibly even contemplate. You have no right to talk to me about ethics."

"Please note that if you don't pay, you will be breaching the boundaries of your employment. It is my recommendation to Tommy that we can... and will... pursue this to the limit."

"So now you're the legal and HR expert as well? Of course, it is your recommendation! It suits your agenda to have me smeared. You forget that I have worked with Tommy, on a daily basis for ten and a half years, without so much as a long weekend! Whatever makes you think you have Tommy's ear over mine?"

"Proximity deary," he said with snide condescension. "I'm here and you're not."

❦❦❦

27.

Stanzie couldn't settle. She couldn't dismiss the fact that Reg might have a point to make, and the means to make it. What if Tommy did go with the loudest voice in his ear? Everything she knew about Reg had the appearance of glowing and good: his enthusiasm was endearing; his understanding of the clients' needs shrewd; his stroking of Tommy's ego, subtle. He did what was required, and while there were visible eyes around, he was sure to do sufficiently extra. Only sometimes, he did let his façade drop and his scathing opinions became aired. Reg's strength was marketing; and he certainly knew how to sell himself. He was a showboat masquerading as a tug. His declaration of team was fraudulent rhetoric. In all of Mac's years of playing hard ball, she had never encountered such blatant ambitions that were so dismissive of the basic tenets of mateship. While someone was useful, you were Reg's best buddy, but if there was a threat of diverting the spotlight off himself, then he dropped you instantly. This was going well beyond abandoning a member of your regiment. It was sabotage. Reg use of terms such as 'embezzlement', 'pursuing it to the limit', 'professional boundaries' had her spooked. She contacted her solicitor and had them to draft up a reply.

What shocked Mac even more than Reg's barefaced vindictiveness, was Tommy complicit agreement. Tommy knew her; worked with her. This betrayal was greater than anything Reg could dish up. Mac knew Reg was dodgy. But Tommy? Tommy was more than a boss. He was the one who encouraged her as a graduate. He was the one who stretched and pushed her. He was the one she allowed to stretch and push her. When clients applied pressure, she had consistently applied the principle that the client was always right, so that Tommy didn't have to choose. She hadn't considered Tommy a weak person, but now she wondered. What if he had not listened to her as a respected equal or professional colleague, but just because she had been the closest, most assertive voice at hand? She hated that she doubted Tommy like this. Had their relationship really only worked because she was a consistent and familiar sounding board? Proximity, Reg said. How meaningless was that?

In those ten years, while the business had grown, she had believed in their team. They were family almost. Certainly, Mac had given more time to the business than anything her family ever got out of her. Even her mum didn't get more than her allocated carer's leave and time-in-lieu. Part of that commitment was listening to Tommy talk. She couldn't count the times he spoke about going out to his hut. The fishing never seemed that good, but the stories generated out there were. He might have gone three or four times, and only ever in quiet spells. Why would he go there now when they were down a person?

She could only assume that Reg was pushing ideas around in his head. Who knew how deep his ambitions ran?

Was he after the whole firm? If Tomlin couldn't see it, or he wasn't going to fight for what they had built, where did that leave her? She couldn't be sure.

♥∞)(∞♥

One morning Jay came and stood sheepishly with his hands in his pockets. He stammered a little and hesitated as Stanzie was organising the day's work. He obviously had something on his mind. Stanzie closed her eyes and wondered if the coaxing and coaching she had offered was going to back-fire. If the kid had a teenage crush on her, here was one seriously broken heart coming up. "C-c-can I sh-sh-show you some-th-thing?"

"Jay, we have a lot to do to get ready for today. Ernie will be here soon. Make it quick."

With a flash of gratitude, he quickly dug deep into his pockets and pulled out a printed sheet of paper, folded and refolded. "I f-f-found this," he said as he shoved it into her hands, restlessly shuffling on the spot. If he had written some outpouring of affection, she would have to try very hard not to flip out.

Stanzie unfolded it impatiently and tried to ignore the harping in her head that wanted to keep distractions to a minimum. She didn't even look at him. "Jay... you found this? What were you thinking?"

His face veiled over. He went silent. "No m-m-matter..."

"No matter? This is amazing! When I asked what you were thinking, I was actually asking what you were thinking. I don't think it's silly. Not at all."

Light dawned in his eyes. "O-o-over th-th-there..." She followed the direction he pointed. "You think we should try something like this over here?"

He nodded enthusiastically. She went for a pencil and realised she didn't have one. They went back to the donga and had a work meeting on the chairs outside. She carefully laid his little printed sheet down. It was a picture of a garden wall inlaid with a stone mosaic of a tree. She pulled out her art book. "What I see developing from this idea is something like this. Cut out an alcove into the path along here... a bench seat like Dan makes... another like the other one down by the willow tree if I can afford it, if not... just a garden variety one... but behind it... extend the wall up like this... and put this mosaic into it. But not any tree... the willow tree. Like this." She considered and then flipped the page. "Or we could put a smaller version of it along here... which is closer to your original idea I think..." She showed him her sketches and asked, "Which one do you like?" She looked up, surprised he seemed subdued. "Are you okay?"

"Y-y-you are so damn c-c-clever. Yet you l-l-like my idea."

"It's a good idea. You knew it was a good idea too. That's why you showed it to me."

"I knew it was g-g-good." He was trying that on for size. He grinned. It seemed to fit.

"Yep. Let's get Dan's opinion. Good ideas grow when we throw them around."

She went over to Dan and showed him Jay's printout, and her sketches. "We have an idea that Jay's come up with, and I think it's got potential. I wanted your opinion: which one?" She watched his face for cues. Too much? Too little?

Dan looked at Jay, and nodded his congratulations. He handed Stanzie back her book. "It's like you said, makes functional interesting... particularly like the idea of the willow theme continuing along the path. I'd probably move this alcove with the seat up to here though, so that you get the longer view of both the house and willow, and then back across the paddocks as well. Yep. I'll give it a tick."

"We weren't going to do both of them."

"Oh. Well." He tapped the larger alcove. "I think that would work. Great idea Jay. Although both would be complimentary and offer balance." And he went back to work.

Now it was her turn to be subdued. She showed the amended concept drafts to Ernie and had the project quote amended accordingly. It was a good idea; everything she knew about design resonated with the landscaping plan. So, what was bugging her?

"Why are you always so dismissive when I ask your opinion? I wonder why I bother!" Ernie and Jay had left for the day. Dan had just come down to where Stanzie was still working in the garden. She stood up and charged him.

"Sorry?"

"I went up there today with the expressed purpose of getting your feedback, and you just dismiss me like a schoolgirl."

"Seriously? My recollection is that you asked for my opinion, and I gave my opinion. It wasn't even negative. What's the problem?"

"My problem is that you hardly said anything. That is not feedback."

"I didn't say enough? That's your problem? What can I say? I'm a man of few words."

"That is such a cop-out. It's just lazy."

"So now I'm lazy. Would hate to see what diligent looks like in your book since I've been diagnosed as a 'pathological workaholic'."

"I'm not talking about your work; but your opinions. That was anything but constructive."

"I offered what I thought was an improvement... which I assume is the benchmark for constructive. And, of course, you get to choose to adopt it, or not, as your whim dictates. Which obviously is the criteria here because you are not making sense. At all."

"Don't turn this on me. I'm just saying that when I ask for feedback, I would appreciate a little more consideration in taking such a request seriously." Had she been hoping that Dan would become her new Tommy, bouncing ideas around, making a partnership of high-minded creative proportions?

"And I'm saying, I did take it seriously."

"But it wasn't just for me. It was for Jay. That kid is so lacking confidence, a few words of encouragement could make a big difference. I give you an opening you could drive a truck through, and still you close off and shut down. Have you nothing else you would say?"

"About your wall?"

"About anything!"

"So, this is not about the wall... or Jay."

"I am just over everything being so minimalistic. It's like pulling teeth. I never know where I stand with you. Why won't you talk to me?"

"I think we are."

"We are what?"

"Talking."

"Then why don't you say anything?"

"I am."

"No, you're not, as usual. I'm not getting any help here, at all. I'm doing all the work. It's supposed to be fifty-fifty!"

He stepped towards her. "Well, aside from the fact that the Little Red Hen asked to do it alone, is it the talking that's important, or the message?"

She sighed impatiently. "Oh, good grief! Of course, that's the point."

He took another step towards her. "I've heard words are less than ten per cent of communicating a message."

"That is ridiculous..." She looked at him uncertain, the force of her barrage fading as she watched him step forward.

"I'm guessing not. But since you asked, I do have some feedback. But it may not be articulate, or wordy or witty. Just a minimalistic take on what I'm thinking... feeling..." A little closer.

"Well, I don't feel it is open between us at all."

"It could be awkward. It may not come out as I intend. I could be judged... unfairly, on the grounds of not being eloquent and clever..." He had slowly closed in. He lifted her chin and he looked into her eyes. She blinked. "Constance, I have some feedback. Not many words. Want to hear it?"

She stood frozen and managed to nod faintly. "Okay..."

He reached out and held her hands, covered in leather work-gloves. He searched her face, holding her with his gaze. She blinked. "Constance, I love your work." And then he gently took off her gloves and kissed her hands, softly. "I love your creativity." He kissed her forehead lightly. "I love your attention to detail." And again. "I love your persistence. I love your laugh. I love your energy. I love your depth. I love your tears. I love that you ask my opinion. I love that you listen to new ideas... and then take them and make them a hundred times better. I love the rhythm that we have when we work together. I love all that." He grinned slightly, softly. "The idea of the stone mosaic, honestly: looks great. And I didn't miss that Jay is craving approval, but sometimes less is more. He heard what I said and that's enough until we tell him again, next time. But what I realised most about the wall, what I loved more than the idea itself, was that if you took on that willow mosaic project, it will take more time. And that got my attention. The timeframe you allocated for staying here is fast running out... and anything that potentially will extend the time I have with you... anything at all... even a bad idea, I may enthusiastically endorse, just because I want you to stay. I would love you to stay. I really want you to stay..." He kissed her, definitely, decisively on the lips and then took three steps back. "See. I can give feedback. Nothing schoolgirl about that."

She stood silent for quite a while. Finally, she took a breath. "So, are you saying the willow-wall concept is a good one? Or just a way to extend the time-line?"

"Conveniently... it is good idea. Ticks both boxes." He paused. After a while he said, "And you... do you have any feedback on my feedback?"

"Speechless..." The irony was not lost on her.

He looked at her thoughtfully. "Hmm. I see. I might go then." And he left.

❧✽❧

28.

Stanzie woke to someone banging on her door. She quickly flicked on the light and checked her phone. Who? Who would be at her door at this hour? She quickly threw on a dressing-gown and ran her hands through her hair as she opened the door.

Stanzie stared at Iris standing there, and her heart started to thump. "Oh goodness, Iris! Come in. Are you okay? You look terrible. What's wrong?"

"Oh, Dear I am so sorry to bother you. I am really quite upset. I haven't slept a wink."

"What on earth is the matter?" Stanzie moved some magazines and cushions to make space on the lounge and then automatically went to click on the jug.

"Dan..."

"Dan?"   Something in her chest stopped beating. "What about Dan?" She went pale... and she leaned hard on the bench. "Is he okay?"

"I don't know. I don't know. He hasn't come home. And I know that he is his own person, and I am not to smother him... but I was hoping... well, I thought maybe his truck might be here, but obviously not. If it was, I would have just gone. I would have let you have your privacy of course. I've been trying to give you both space. I've tried to ring, and I've left messages. Normally he would let me know, and he's been so steady and not done these erratic things at all for such a long time... and I'm really worried. Something has happened. Something has happened. I feel it in here..."

Stanzie handed her a cup of tea and saw Iris's hands tremble as she took it. Oh yes, she thought, something has happened. Something undeniably has happened. She felt her chest constrict, just like the morning she woke up and Dad was not in the kitchen drinking his morning beer. "Where might he go? Do you have any idea?" Stanzie asked.

Suddenly Iris looked very, very old. She stared at Stanzie through her glasses and shrugged. "I just thought you might know. Did you have a fight?"

Stanzie blinked. "No... I don't think so..."

"You didn't? Thank God. I thought perhaps he might take it bad if you turned him down. He's totally smitten with you dear. You do know that?" Stanzie nodded. Yes, she knew that. Now. "Dan is so much like my Dave... one hundred per cent in. No half measures. Once he's in, he's in."

"Oh..." Stanzie groaned as the possibilities enlarged in the shadows.

Iris looked at her, the pupils unusually large through the lenses of her glasses. "What happened?" she whispered.

"Oh Iris. I didn't say anything. I couldn't. I was stunned. I've been just lying there thinking and thinking about what he said... and I've must have dozed off... but I..." She shrugged. Helpless.

"He told you how he feels?" She nodded.

"And you don't love him?" Iris pressed her for an answer.

"Oh! I don't know. I'm terrified. Terrified that he is not okay; that something has happened; that he won't be here; that he's changed his mind; that I won't get to do what we did yesterday, tomorrow or the day after... and the day after that. He said he wanted me to stay. But I don't know. This wasn't part of the plan."

"Oh, my Dear, you're frightened..." Iris had been revisited by a familiar demon this night and she recognised her own fear precisely. It was strange to her that not everyone would have this same acquaintance with fear.

Stanzie stood up and paced. She'd been pacing all night in her head... and now it was a relief to walk it out. "Damn you, Dan Henry. Why couldn't you leave me alone? I was doing okay. I was doing fine."

"But Dear, you weren't doing fine. That's why you came here. To work it out..."

"Yes, but not like this. It was just supposed to be me. I don't need a knight in shining armour. I'm okay; I can work it out. I don't need anyone to rescue me. I can't. They leave. They always leave." Tears welled in Stanzie's eyes, and she sat down, wrapping her arms around her shoulders, holding herself very still.

"Oh. I see." And Iris sat back against a cushion and closed her eyes, sipped her tea... and prayed.

Finally, Stanzie stirred. "I didn't want this. I didn't flirt with him. Do you think I led him on? Oh goodness... is that...? I mean I wondered. I liked the idea that he respects my work, or that he might find me... interesting... or like he said... that our work has rhythm. He just knows how I work. I had a go at him... about not taking me seriously. I thought men don't talk about stuff because they don't do feelings. But Dan... he has amazing insight. I just don't understand why he doesn't talk to me about those things. I think I was hoping that we would not just be a working team... but a creative team... but it didn't come out that way at all. When he told me how he felt, I realised I was so off base, and to be honest, that shocked me. I couldn't think of anything to say. But then... he just left. He didn't insist I respond. He just left. And now I don't know if he changed his mind; or whether he's taken off because I didn't say anything. I don't know..." Suddenly the free-flowing stream of thought dried up.

She took a deep breath and gathered a couple of empty mugs to take to the sink, just because it gave her a reason to create motion.

She looked over at Iris who sat on the lounge blinking in the lamplight. "He'd better not go and do anything stupid. If he does, I'll..." Stanzie sat down at the table and put her head on her arms and sighed. Frank-L came and put her head in her lap. Suddenly she stood up, swiping her face. "Boy he's tenacious. The number of times I was sure he had pulled out... but he was always there. And to start with I only wanted him there... for work, because it would have been so inconvenient if he went. But..." She stared at Iris in a moment of revelation... and swore slowly. "I've been like this for months, haven't I? I don't want him to just be my builder." She sat down slowly like she had seen a ghost. "I didn't even realise. But I'm terrified. That's not right. I thought about what Smithy said: that perfect love casts out fear. If that's the case, being scared surely is not the way it is meant to be. He's like a tick or something that's been burrowing under my skin... irritating the hell out of me. I can't think of anything else! He makes me so furious!"

Iris looked into her cup. "Yes Dear, I know. I married his father. It was the same with him."

"I had no idea it was like this. Did you always love Dave? Was it easy for you?"

"Easy? No... I wouldn't call it easy. I ran. He followed me to England, of all places."

Stanzie grimaced a little. "Some people call that stalking."

"Some people. But it wasn't like that with Dave. I realised I felt safer when we were together than when we were apart. Didn't matter whether we were fighting or not.

I don't mean abusive-yelling-hitting-screaming-fighting... but finding how to survive the tension... how to express our differences. It took a while to learn that. We got better at it. In the end we didn't need to fight at all. It was okay to disagree, to think differently. He was the most trustworthy man. Life with him was like a bubble... a safe, loving bubble." Her cup rattled in the saucer as she put it down and she looked up at Stanzie. "And you, Dear. Do you trust Dan?"

"Trust?"

"Perhaps you don't need 'trust'. Perhaps for you there is something else..."

"I think... constancy... being there. Not leaving. Why am I just realising that I want him to stay now that he's left?" Stanzie looked at her hand and traced her mother's ring on her finger. "Maybe that was why my Mum was so fixated on my name. Maybe that was what she needed too. Maybe she wanted me to be named for those things: *Constance Charity.* Dependability, steadiness, kindness, love. No conditions, just stability. Oh, my goodness! That's it, isn't it? I didn't want to be those things for my mother. I wanted him to be those things. But he wasn't. He left."

"Just because Dan went without saying something further, does that mean he has none of those qualities?"

"Dan? No. No, Dad. He left. I didn't want to be the constant loving one... I wanted Dad to be that... for Mum and me. But he left. He never wanted any part of it. He never wanted me to be called Constance. So, it was easier to go by the name that didn't remind me of those things either. It was an obligation he never subscribed to. Why should I?"

"Iris looked confused. "It sounds like some dots are joining for you, Dear..."

"It feels like a relief. I think Dan got it. He said I should work out why my name was so uncomfortable for me. I've thought about it... but never quite like this." She looked over at Iris sitting quietly on the lounge holding her cup of tea with her eyes closed like it was keeping her from falling over. "Iris, do you think Dan took my silence as rejection?" Frank-L sat at the door, waiting to be let out.

"Well now. I am dramatic by nature. I panicked. You have been working through things I've not been aware of. Tell me again... what did he say?"

"He said he loved my work... but mostly just me. I was stunned. I didn't... maybe I couldn't say anything. I just stood there like someone had hit me with a plank. Then he just said he was going, and I didn't try to stop him. I should have tried to stop him!"

"Well Dear. We only do what we can at the time. Dan has his own choices to make here. I say that to remind myself mostly. I really did panic. I have frightened you. I'm so sorry. We will have to wait and see what today brings I guess." Iris stood to her feet and wavered a little.

"Oh Iris. Please, can you stay? Until we hear where he is. Please. I don't want to be alone just now. Please have some breakfast... eat something and have a rest before you go. You look exhausted."

"Some toast maybe..."

"Yes. Toast. Good idea. Here, put your feet up. I'm just going to run to the loo, and I'll be back in a minute." The early light of dawn was starting to filter through the curtains on the windows. She paused at the door. "Thank you, Iris. Thank you for not judging my confusion."

"How could I? You are a very dear friend. It is our secret that we were friends long before you even knew I was related to your good-looking builder." She smiled, a cheeky sparkle coming back into her eyes.

"Huh. Why don't relationships come with a guarantee?"

"I think that perhaps if we took out the risk, that would also take out the fun... and the adventure... and the love. What I know of Dan is that if he says something, he means it. Nothing as benign as silence will keep him away. He'll recognise shock when he sees it. And he'll be waiting. I could possibly guarantee that."

Stanzie offered a grateful smile to her very good friend. She was grateful not to be alone in this. "You give me faith to think it might be okay," she said.

As she opened the door, Frank-L pushed past her and smothered Dan in a warm morning welcome. He was sitting on the step and laughed, quickly standing up. He grabbed the rail, supporting Stanzie as she toppled into a tangle of dog and Dan. He held her for a moment, and he kissed her forehead. "You give me faith to think it might be okay too," he said.

Relief flooded her, and she snapped at him, pulling away. "You've just been sitting there!"

His eyes were bright. "Good morning C-C. It just gets better," he said with a grin. "Who knew the Charity Train was not about free-loading at all... Constance Charity?"

"You! You are not even sorry you were listening!"

"But the demountable walls are so thin, and it was so interesting. And to interrupt, would have been rude. I was hoping you would continue a bit longer..."

"Well, I've had a little too much coffee. I will be back in a tick..." Suddenly she went quiet and looked into his eyes. "Dan? Please, don't leave. Please, stay until I get back."

"Go? No chance. I'm here. Even after you get back: I'm staying."

❧ ❧ ❧

29.

Dan had made himself a coffee and put on some toast, and then parked himself on the floor beside his mother, as she lay propped with a cushion on the lounge. Stanzie sat on a chair looking at them. "I don't know whether to hit you or hug you. You frightened your mother to death."

"She looks pretty alive to me." He didn't look at all repentant.

"You didn't answer your phone. Where were you? What happened?"

"Hmm. Just around. Think my phone is still in the ute."

"Stalking?" Huh. Like father, like son.

"Okay. I was down on the bench by the willow tree. I haven't slept either. That tree and I had a lot to talk about. I used to go down there and climb it as a kid when I was trying to lay low. I had some thinking to do."

"Your Mum was worried."

He kind of thought Stanzie was missing the point. His Mum wasn't the only one. "I've had my heart in my throat all night. I thought about coming up a couple of times... but I couldn't."

"Couldn't? Why? Why wouldn't you let us know you were okay?"

"I went for a long drive... And then a long walk. Thought you might have heard me come in."

"Frank-L was restless at one stage. I put that down to my agitation."

"I came up when I saw your light come back on. I went to knock... but, well... I became engrossed in the feedback I didn't get yesterday. There-in lies some relief."

Iris sat up. "You know, I think I might go. You two need some time."

"Stay." They both said together, their eyes locked in on each other.

She looked from one to the other. "You know. I still think I might go. I'll lie down on your bed Stanzie if that's okay. I'm exhausted."

She stood up with her cup of tea and went into the bedroom and firmly closed the door behind her. They had not taken their eyes off each other.

"Did you hear the 'I'm scared' part? I'd hardly call that surety."

"You are right... there is no money back guarantee. This is where I reassure you, I'm not here to rescue you... or to sweep you onto my gallant steed... as appealing as these images are."

"Let me make it clear Dan. I don't need your help. I can do this on my own."

"Suits me. Neediness is over-rated."

"Then what's this about? I don't get it."

"Perhaps, my Little Red Hen, I have come to realise I want to do it with you... not for you. I want to be here in the face of all of the stuff life dishes out. It's not about taking your tears away but being together when we cry."

"When I say I'm scared, I really am..." Her eyes filled, and she turned away.

"I know. Truth be known... I am too. But it hasn't stopped me wanting to take away your fear; or your restlessness; or your tears. I want to see you smile... and only smile." Stanzie swallowed, but before she said anything, he continued. "I know that as chivalrous as these ambitions might be, you are right; I can't do that for you. So instead of trying to fix the things that make problems, I want to be with you to experience all the things life brings."

Stanzie looked at him and her tears spilt over. So much for that self-avowed promise she would never cry in front of him. She had never heard anyone talk about togetherness like that. It felt strange, and gentle, and erotic. He didn't move. He didn't rush to her side. He stayed there, loving her, holding her by being just there and it felt right. So right.

When she dried her tears, he gently said, "I want to start with the little bits and put it all together, so it creates something... something that wasn't there before. Two do-ers, doing it together."

Tears sprung to her eyes, again.   "Damn. We are doomed."

"Why?"

"Because Do-ers leave. My Dad was a do-er. He said that all the time. "I am a do-er, C-C," he'd say. He said that right up until the day before my eighth birthday. Then he was gone. He left to do something better than being family." She couldn't understand her sense of impending doom. Hadn't she been to this place before? Hadn't she sorted this out already? Why did she always come back to this?

"Is that why this Studio is so personal? To do something he didn't... to connect with him somehow?"

"It was supposed to be about saying good-bye to Mum. She really loved the country. But she never got to do that. I guess I wanted something that would be a space where other people could come and do what she missed out on. I thought that perhaps I could learn to appreciate it as well."

"And... is it working?"

"I don't really get what she saw in it. Like the thing about all the bush birds... ha! I'm sure the occasional crow, or sparrow, or fish-eating kookaburra isn't exactly what she was talking about. But I like the open space... and I'm getting very okay with the quiet. When Mum was sick everything was so frantic... we never had time or space for anything but the next treatment or the next appointment. So, I wanted to create a space people could use when there is so much going on for them. But it seems as though all I managed was to just make a different sort of busy. I can't even grieve and not do.

I really am like him. I do. All the time. I'm doing. It's what I do: I do."

He grinned. "You do know all that do-doing sounded quite ridiculous." She threw a cushion at him. He caught it and put it behind his back. "I also know you are not your father. I didn't know him Stanzie... but I know you. And I know me. We have our faults, but we don't have to live under the shadow of someone else's mistakes. He was wrong to leave you Stanzie. He was. But just because he stuffed-up, doesn't mean we can't choose something different. The doing and the leaving are two different things. With God's help we can choose differently. Every day... we choose to stay... we choose to do something different."

"For someone who couldn't give feedback on a drawing, you have plenty to say now."

"I need you to know... after the agony of all this... if you allow me in; if I get to stay, I am not going to leave."

"If? You have wriggled your way in here without me hardly even being aware of it!"

"That sounds parasitic."

She smiled. Relieved. Indulgent. "If the hat fits... Dan, I like working with you. I like that you like working with me. I like that your mother likes me. However, to be honest, I don't like your brother that much; although your nephew is adorable." She came over and sat on the lounge next to him while he was still sitting on the floor. "I like this."

He looked up at her, his chin rough and unshaved. "Like?"

"I haven't liked much in a very long time. This is pretty good progress."

"I love that you like it." He reached up and pulled her off balance until she crumpled into his lap on the floor. "I love that you are working this out. It's okay. I'm not going." He paused. "But I do have a question..." He waited, his eyes expectant.

Oh, here it comes, she thought. "Okay..."

"Constance Charity Macintosh... may I court you? Old fashioned date... woo... fall in love with you?"

"You want to fall in love with me?"

"Nah, you're probably right... no hope on that one." She laughed at him. "You are just weird. Do you know that? I can't, for the life of me, understand you at all. Other guys I've dated would have been trying to get in my pants for months now. I've wondered why I am not attractive to you... that you wouldn't want to."

"Not attractive? Oh! I find you seriously sizzling. That's code for really hot."

"Then why... why do you just want to court me?"

"Believe me, this is not 'just'. It is going somewhere. But this time, I want to do it this way. Please say yes."

"Why? Why not just take it as it comes?"

"Because as-it-comes is less... less interesting. And you... you are so interesting. You deserve interesting."

"I would have thought that was staged, and staid, and constrained, rather than interesting – even by your definition."

Dan shrugged. "Guess it depends how you look at it. Beside if you say yes, you're in on it: fifty-fifty. And that has me fascinated. Really intrigued. What other amazing dates can you come up with?"

"You liked the painting picnic?"

"That will be a hard act to follow, but not impossible. I fear your creativity will be stretched to the limits."

"This is a dubious strategy if you're trying for chivalry. But okay – you are on! Date away. Fifty-fifty."

He sighed. "I am caught out. I've lost before we have started."

Stanzie pulled herself back. "Rubbish. You think this little stunt has got it in the bag for you. Well, I still don't know... and it still has me terrified. But my confidence is this... my creativity has depths that are yet to be plumbed. Dan Henry, you may have just bitten off more than you can chew."

He looked at her with a smile in his eyes that he made no attempt to mask. "I think it just got interesting," and he pulled her in for a kiss.

ॐ⊙⊗

30. Epilogue

Dan opened the door to his ute. "I've kind of got to confess something." He seemed a little embarrassed. Stanzie looked at him curiously as he continued sheepishly. "You were right. I admit I've bitten off more than I can chew. I've run out of ideas for our dates."

"But the rule is fifty-fifty. You cannot simply admit defeat. It's not in the courtly code."

"This is supposed to be my heartfelt, vulnerable confession. There is no code for that."

"Alright. Sorry. Go ahead. Confess away."

"Okay. So,... I wanted to apologise ahead of time that today's outing is not an original idea. And no matter how hard I've tried; I realise you've out done me. So,... I thought I would revisit an old one." He shrugged and mouthed, "Sorry."

"Gee, Daniel, I don't know. Can I go out with you if it's not original, interesting, and mysterious? This is our brief. You're not keeping up your end of the bargain."

He frowned and screwed up his eyes. "Yeah. I know. Just wanted to give you the heads up, so you will not be disappointed and will forgive me. Although I will say, of all our mysterious and exhilarating adventures, this particular date was my favourite."

"Which one?" She peeked into the back of the ute. No hints there.

"Oh no. I'm not giving that up just yet."

"Hmm. Now I'm curious. I'm not dressed for rock climbing..."

"What you have on is fine."

"Okay then... less active. Dinner under the willow arbour..."

"No moonlight at eleven a.m. That was good though."

"Less romantic. Ahh. Making the bench seat in your shed..."

"Hmm. I do admit the wine and cheese were a nice touch. No, that's not it."

"Fishing?" she suggested tentatively.

He laughed. "You are no good at this game at all. That was a disaster. We argued the whole time!"

"True... The... ahh. No. I've got nothing. Theatre?" He shook his head and yawned. She shrugged. "I'm done."

"Fair enough. But in trying to salvage a vestige of the mysterious, I will have to blind-fold you. Feel free to guess as we go. Although I am allowed to lie through my teeth if you get close."

"Since when? You are not allowed to lie! What sort of Christian man are you?"

"A desperate one... who has run out of ideas."

"Pathetic shabby affair, I would say."

"Point taken. No peeking. I just have to grab some things so we will stop every so often." He went to the Servo to pick up a box of things he had left there. It included a picnic rug and basket that Iris had prepared. Next, he pulled into a parking lot, got out and stared at the sky tapping his foot for a few minutes, before getting back in breathless. "Just one more stop, and then we should just about be there..." He randomly pulled over on the side of the road. Got out again, went behind a tree and then got back in adjusting his fly.

"What are you getting at all these places? You don't seem at all organised Dan. It is not like you to be so sluggish in your dates."

"Yeah, sorry about that. Last minute. Been a busy week."

"Huh. Really? Busy week? No more than usual and no more than mine. That's poor." Yet she privately admitted her irritation was not very deep and she was actually enjoying the distraction from the heaviness of her reflections that were dogging her. "Are we there yet?"

"Oh! I knew you wouldn't be able to do this without using that line. You have the attention span of a four-year-old."

"Or the constitution of one. The motion is starting to mess with me."

"Nearly there. Seriously. Two minutes. Can you hold on?"

"Yep. Make it quick."

"We are here..." He slowed down and then pulled up. "Stay there. I'm coming around..." He jumped out and opened the door for her. Led her out, steadying her arm in her disorientation. "How are you feeling?"

"A bit queasy... but okay. Where are we?"

He held her blindfold, turned her around and then gently took off the scarf. "We're here..."

"Oh! My beautiful Old Lady! This was your favourite date? Really?"

"I even stole your painting things yesterday... in case you are inclined..."

She laughed. "You are having a moral crisis Dan. Lazy, lying... now thievery..."

"Yeah. I notice you look really concerned about that. I brought brunch." They laid out the rug and contents of basket. There was a blanket of petals under the jacaranda tree, framing the view in spectacular tones of purple.

"I might sit and enjoy this for a while. I still feel a bit disorientated."

"Given the remarkable ideas you had about where we might be headed, you were totally lost by the time we got to the intersection at the servo."

"Very clever." She turned to look at the tumbled old house again. "Oh Dan. They've sold her!" She spotted an Under Contract sign near the steps. Look. Oh. That's kind of nice, I guess... and sad. Who would have thought that after all these years, someone would want her?"

"Yeah. I heard. Guess I wanted to remember her like this."

"Perhaps she will be loved again after all this time. Gee, I'm feeling a little nostalgic. We only came here once."

"Maybe this wasn't a good idea after all. I didn't intend to evoke melancholy and misery."

"Very poetic. No this is great. She is so lovely," she said gazing at the ruined lines of the house veiled elegantly in tints of mauve from the flowering trees.

"Hmm. Not only her..." He paused, and then quickly picked up a glass. "Here... some soda-water?"

She twirled a purple bloom in her fingers as she took the stemmed glass. She raised her drink, and smiled pensively, "To classic beauty, to elegance and past glories." They clinked glasses and drank pensively.

"Do you know what I liked about that date?" Dan stretched out on the rug.

"You saw my talent unveiled?" He rolled his eyes and she laughed at him.

"It was our first real date. In fact, I believe I fell in love with you sitting here at this very spot."

"Really? Here? Then? Why?"

"You were painting, and dreaming, and laughing all afternoon. You are so talented and yet it was the first time I saw you, really saw you without that compulsive need to dogmatically advocate for yourself."

"Compulsively blowing my trumpet. Sounds terrible..." She cringed.

"...just sitting there, painting, blushing self-consciously. Adorable."

"I remember being very uncomfortable... and I don't know how many times you said it was all part of the deal. I tried to ignore you, and just paint... but your presence was so loud!

"I never said a word!"

"Well, I couldn't ignore you... and I didn't want to be seen as reneging. I couldn't let you to think you were getting the upper hand. So, I had to stick it out. I'm a little competitive by nature."

"A little? And then... Hang on a minute." He went to the ute and brought back the canvas. "Remember this?" He passed it to her, and she held it, smiling wistfully.

"Who is nostalgic now? Yes... Not badly executed given the stress I was under. It was fun actually. I've not done painting outdoors since I was a kid doing art lessons."

"You called it 'My Lady's Dream'. You captured that moment of us on the rug... the parasol shading your face and me with boater and braces, even the unopened book. The phases of life... the passage of time... and then it moves into a vision of a hopeful future."

Stanzie traced the old lodge, as it might have been, with her finger, and moved across the canvas into the dilapidated timbers of now, which led into the dream of what could be. That was what Dan had invited her to see. The ghost of the past, transforming a ruined present into this vision of something grand and beautiful, again. "Hopeful? I think it's sad. Listen to the wind through her broken eaves. I can hear her sighing over that broken dream. It's the most lost, mournful sound…"

"Some things are beautiful enough to mourn, I think, if they never come to be."

"It's been sort of metaphorical for me, this picture. Perhaps it's really My Dream. But who can tell what the future can hold? It was so clear… what we dreamt that day. I could see that. But now? It's fuzzy. I don't know what's next. I've extended my time as long as I can. I'm doing some jobs part-time, but Tommy's getting edgy. He wants an answer about me coming back, but I don't know if I can. Not full-time at least."

"Where's the hesitation?"

"The whole flavour of the place has changed. I don't want to default to that just because it's all I've ever done."

"That's what you don't want. What is it that you want?"

She shrugged. "That is the million-dollar question. I love what I do. I'm good at it. But now? I don't know. I'm trying to work out if I'm just ticked off because I'm not Tommy's favourite anymore since Reg's become the Chosen One. That whole invoice thing: that was a debacle. Tommy backed right down once I stood up to Reg's bullying. Suddenly he was very accommodating, trying to smooth things over. That job used to be such a good fit… and I'm so frustrated that it is not like that anymore."

"You're talking in past-tense. Have you left already?"

"Perhaps. I know I don't trust Reg as far as I can spit, and I certainly don't want to work with him. If he wasn't there it would be simpler, but when Tommy swapped out so easily, it makes me really doubt I can work with him; the way I used to anyway. Don't know what happened to 'Don't want to lose you, Mac!' I thought loyalty was a value we both held, but that was betrayal. It's not the same now. I know Reg wants me out and I really don't want him to win; but I feel that if I go back, I lose anyway. I want to explore something different I guess, but there are not too many options for doing what I do, without moving to a large centre."

"Perhaps 'The Willow Studio' has given you a taste of what different can look like."

"Yeah, but it's over now. I'm sad it's over, but I can't stay in this role of doing therapeutic remodelling forever. I have finished what I came here to achieve. It is beautiful. It really is. It's everything that I saw. The gardens are just about done. But for all our talking, I haven't been able to nail it down. I've tried to make a plan... yet nothing sits right."

"Did you know today is our anniversary? Twelve months ago, I was sitting at Snooks' servo drinking coffee, praying you'd spit the dummy and choose another builder."

"You were praying me away! You never told me that. I'm not surprised though. I could tell you didn't like me."

"Some things change. I've changed. If you chose another builder now, I'd be devastated." She looked at him. He looked uneasy.

"Dan, when I say I don't know, I know you are in my future. I can't see it any other way. I'm just talking about what happens next. I don't know that."

"Well, I've got something that might be an idea. If you like it... we'll give it a go. If not, we'll make a different plan. This is for you." He handed her a gift, wrapped simply in plain blue paper.

"An anniversary present?" She looked curiously at the serious expression on Dan's face. "This means a lot to you, doesn't it?"

"You have no idea..."

Inside was a large thick envelope. Not quite the usual gift. She broke the seal tentatively and pulled out a wad of documents tied firmly with a burgundy ribbon.

There, secured in the bow, on a golden thread, was a gold and diamond ring. "Marry me, Constance," he said as she touched it curiously... turning it, rolling the diamond to catch the sunlight. "Make this the next thing..."

She went still, staring at it glinting. His heart began pounding; had he misread the pace of their relationship? Did she not desire this too? They had talked about this. God, what if she says 'No'? He hadn't factored a No.

"You want to do this? Now?"

"I really do."

"This is not just because you've run out of ideas, and you don't want to date me anymore?" Her face was serious.

He met her gaze, his face equally solemn. "I am so done dating. I want to marry you."

"But... there remains that fear-factor." She paused and looked away with tears in her eyes. "I thought that would go away, but it hasn't. Not completely. Perhaps it is like you said: facing the unknown. So, I feel... I would have to say... 'Yes'." She smiled through the mist. "Yes, I'll marry you Dan. Let's face the fear together... let's do the unknown, together."

"Oh, my goodness! You just sent me into a tailspin! Talk about fear-factor." He pulled her in for a kiss that was deep and passionate. He placed the ring on her finger and smiled. "I am so relieved you think it is a good plan," he said. Then he pointed to the papers. "And the rest? What do you think about that?"

She laughed. "All your fumbling and stopping! There is nothing last minute about any of this: you've even included paperwork. Nice touch."

She unfolded the documents. Surely there wasn't an 'Intent to Marry' form? That would be the least romantic gesture that could be applied to an otherwise perfect proposal. She read the top page. There was a muted photograph of the old house that featured a spectacular sunset behind it. "Memorabilia. Something to remember her by," she whispered. That was an improvement at least. With it was some Real Estate propaganda: a nice little blurb about great potential; renovator's dream; handyman's special; needs TLC. She chuckled. "I hope whoever bought it doesn't seriously think it can be renovated. Bulldozer opportunity." She flipped the page and stared at the mortgage deed. "You! You bought this? You bought the Grand Old Lady? That 'Under Contract' sign is yours?"

Dan nodded. "Ours. I like to think of it as liberating her. My idea was more along the lines of this." He held up the canvas, so it superimposed the view of the house. "This elegant vestige of the past is also part of our family history. It used to be the main homestead of the original Gumleigh Station. This was the block that Irvin Guthrie thought he had bought when he moved here. He was conned into signing a contract believing this was what he had purchased. But what he got instead was that other rocky little block that was, for all intents and purposes, good for nothing. It was just the overseer's cottage then, but it wasn't long before that residence was replaced by this homestead. It has caused so much controversy in our family down the years. The greatest controversy was that Mum married into that family. Dad brought me here and told me the story. I think, he wanted to instil the idea that ambition should never substitute respect and integrity. I'm not trying to right the wrong made against the Guthries by buying this, but I think I want to reclaim the idea that both are possible: ambition with integrity works better."

"There it is again: function marries interesting... not compromising on style or ethics for a price-tag. Both need to live side by side.

"Old Mr Guthrie, my great-great Grandfather, would appreciate the irony. Bizarre really; how things come around. If my memory serves me correctly, you said you wanted to be married here. I thought that idea was inspired. Whether we just go with the view... or wait until later, there's no hurry to decide. It's ours."

"Have I ever told you, I love working with you? So much. So very, very much."

"Love?"

"I haven't loved much in a very long time. This is exponential progress."

"I love that we are building something. This is not just the Grand Old Lady. We are putting together something significant... taking notice of the past, using that to inform our present, to create something new and interesting and good for the future."

Tears prickled behind her eyes. "I am so blessed. I get to do family with you Dan. Being family. I never thought something that interesting would happen for me."

He leaned in and they kissed again. "You are beyond interesting... more like intriguing – that's interesting on a whole 'nother level!"

Peace settled over her as she leaned back and gazed up into the branches of the jacaranda tree... so different from the willow's contorted posture. Her crying was done. These limbs were strong, dressed in their royal purple blooms, swaying gently inviting her to stand up tall. "It's perfect," she sighed. "Perfect. Doing life... being together."

ॐ≈ঞৎ≈

The end

More Books by this Author

Stand-alone Stories

Matt's Boys of Wattle Creek

When Matthew Lawson's three sons were born, he wrote each of them a letter outlining his hopes and prayers for their futures. When he decided to give up his city job and move to the little town of Wattle Creek, he could never have imagined the effect it would have on his young family. As Matt's boys grow to maturity and find their places in their community, will his dreams and prayers come to fulfilment? Will his boys develop their own faith in the eternal God? And will they each find the kind of love that Matt holds for his beautiful Josie?

Maggie & Minotaur

"For Maggie, the mythical Minotaur represented Romance – half man, half beast. The Minotaur was a monster created from centuries of classical Greek mythology and no normal man could withstand its strength…… Sooner or later she would accept that Theseus, the hero, did not exist. She knew that she would have to battle through the maze of reality and confront it herself…." Maggie Wick was shipped off to the city and high society life at the age of 12, where she would learn the ways of the rich and marry into a family of influence. What could have caused her sudden return to Henderson's Gap? Can she really settle back into life on the station, with all its diversity and challenges? Will she find fulfilment in her role as provisional schoolteacher? Will she ever figure out the "Captain", the mysterious, intimidating, station manager? When war comes to her little haven and Maggie's world comes crashing down, taking her loved ones and the captain with it, Maggie needs to find a way to survive. Will her faith be enough to protect her, and what of the Captain? Could he really be the Theseus who would do battle with her Minotaur?

#1 The Beachside Cottage

In this offering from Olwyn Harris, we meet the heartbroken and downtrodden Eliza-Beth Perkins. Eliza-Beth is facing the dire consequences of her choices and the possibility of life in the poorhouse. Then she, literally, runs into Jensen Harker. Jensen is facing his own heartbreak at the death of his wife and wants nothing more than to be left alone. But something in Eliza-Beth stirs him to make a rash proposal, thus rescuing her from her predicament. As we follow their journey together, will we see them find the healing they both desperately need?

#2 Petrea Downs

In the 2nd book in this series, we meet Meg. Meg's life has been turned upside-down, with her husband gone, trying to run Petrea Downs by herself, and disaster after disaster at every turn. Thankfully, her neighbour Everett Grossman is always there to help. The final blow comes when a cattle duffer tries to steal her only source of income, gets shot, and has to be nursed back to health in her living room. But, is Ben Harker really the villain he seems? And is Everett really the hero he makes himself out to be?

#3 The Writer's Retreat

The third book in the Homes of Healing trilogy introduces us to Tess, a romance writer, who prides herself on letting her characters tell their own story. When she arrives at Rocky Creek B&B, the run-down stone cottage looks like the perfect place for her to retreat to, not only to write her book, but to escape her past. Join her as she discovers her characters and explores their stories, and finds that God is intent on becoming part of her own story at the same time. As her relationship with the local publican challenges her to stop running, she realises that real life and real love can be messy and complicated. Can she honestly confront the ugly aspects in her own story, so that God can bring them both to a place of healing?

#1 Sapphires of Hope

"There is no way," she thought, "that I am going to use this!" She had desperately searched their cupboards for something, anything that would come close to what she needed for her catering project. She found only this old dilapidated breadbasket that looked like the sort of junk that comes from one of those tacky jumble-sale stalls..."

Andi and Jo are best friends... they do pretty much everything together. So, when Andi has a catering assignment due, and only a tacky old basket to use, Jo helps her pull off the faded decorations, revealing a time-capsule of historical information, and in order to understand what it means, Andi and Jo ask their elderly neighbour to take them to visit the farm where the basket came from. They find themselves dumped back in history at the time of Federation, embroiled in circumstances that nearly cost Andi her life and threatens the livelihood of the people living there. How can they ever hope to keep going when things are spinning out of control?

#2 Rubies of Ambition

In the 2nd book in the Gem of Australia series, we again travel with Andi and Jo back in time. On this adventure, they meet the very beautiful and ambitious actress, Lillian Browning, who is on the run from the federal police. Andi and Jo accompany her back to her home town, where they find she is not well received. Will Lillian find a balance between the past that calls her and the ambitions that drive her?

#1: A Spacious Place

In this first instalment of the Guthrie's Lot series, set in the late 1800s, we meet Irvin Guthrie, a practical, no-nonsense man with a sick wife and a small child to care for. When his wife's doctor suggests they move to a warmer climate, he spends everything he has on a property that ends up not being what he expected.

Joanna Grenham has dreams of being a school teacher. When an opportunity presents itself, she jumps at the chance, only to find herself given no choice but to care for Irvin's sick wife and child.

Will Irvin and Joanna make the most of their circumstances, or will they forever find life as hard and unyielding as the ground in A Spacious Place.

#2: A Level Path

In the second instalment of the Guthrie's Lot series, it is now the late 1960s. Here we meet Irvin's granddaughter Iris. Iris hungers for excitement and adventure, and she won't find that in Gumleigh, or with the ever predictable Dave. The last thing she expected was for Dave to follow her across the world to England as she tries to find direction and meaning.

Will Iris finally see through the charismatic, but ultimately selfish, Stan, or will Dave leave England alone and leave Iris to find her own way to A Level Path?

Children's Stories

The Bush Olympics

The Bush Olympics, written by Olwyn Harris and beautifully illustrated by Shelly Askew, shows us that we don't have to be good at everything to be part of a team. Even sleepy Koala is good at something, and if everyone plays their part, we can all be successful together.

More titles from Olwyn Harris coming soon.